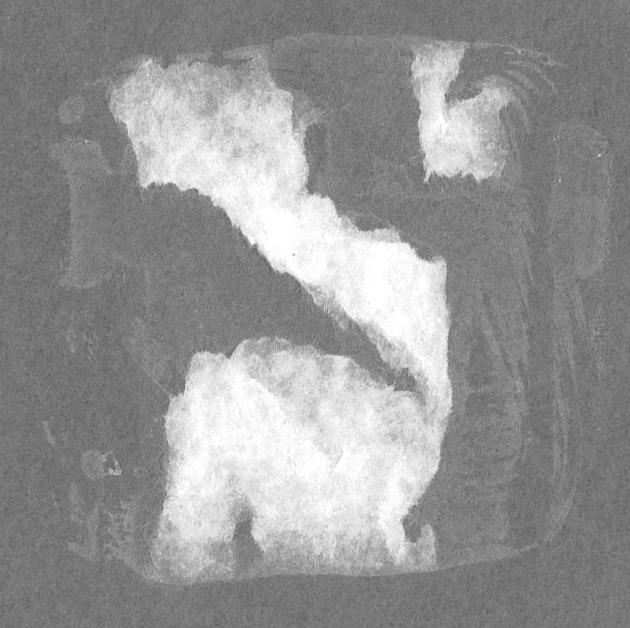

BALYET

Also by Patricia Wrightson

THE ICE IS COMING
THE DARK BRIGHT WATER
JOURNEY BEHIND THE WIND
A LITTLE FEAR
THE NARGUN AND THE STARS
MOON DARK

BALYET

Patricia Wrightson

Margaret K. McElderry Books
NEW YORK

Published in May 1989 by
British Century Hutchinson Group Ltd

Margaret K. McElderry Books
Macmillan Publishing Company
866 Third Avenue
New York, NY 10022

First United States Edition
Printed in the United States of America
10 9 8 7 6 5 4 3 2 1

Composition by Haddon Craftsmen
Allentown, Pennsylvania
Printed and bound by R. R. Donnelley & Sons
Harrisonburg, Virginia
Designed by Barbara A. Fitzsimmons

Library of Congress Cataloging-in-Publication Data
Wrightson, Patricia.
Balyet.
Summary: Despite the precautions of the old aborigine woman she calls Granny, fourteen-year-old Jo falls under the spell of a secret thing in the Australian hills, a girl endlessly alive and crying for the death that will not take her.
[1. Supernatural—Fiction. 2. Australian aborigines—Fiction. 3. Australia—Fiction] I. Title.
PZ7.W9593Bal 1989 [Fic] 88-8298
ISBN 0-689-50468-3

Author's Note

The legend of Balyet was recorded by Mrs. Ethel Hassell in the 1880s, in her manuscript published by C. W. Hassell in 1975 under the title My Dusky Friends. *This is Balyet's story; it is not the story of Jo, Terry, Lance, or Kevin.*

Mrs. Willet, as an aboriginal Australian and a Clever Woman, has a better right to the story, since she inherits the laws and traditions that made it. There were Clever Women as well as Clever Men among her People, as there were much later in English villages, which depended for help and healing on local witches or wizards and called them Clever Women or Clever Men.

Though this is Balyet's story, its development and ending are, of course, mine. Like other legendary figures more widely known but mostly less moving, Balyet is evergreen and her story has no ending.

BALYET

1

THE HILLS SPRANG UP FROM THE PLAIN three thousand feet in one leap: from outflung ridges, up worn and chiseled heights, to bare faces of rock flying against the sky. At their feet lay the scrub-covered coastal plain, diminished into irrelevance; only the hills had meaning. Lifting their heads above shadowed gullies, they gazed over the plain, beyond the far edge of the continent, to the cold south seas out of which the autumn came.

Forests and winds were caught in them. Birds winged up and down their heights. Wallabies traveled them by ledges and invisible tracks. Death and sorrow lived there too, but the hills did not see them. The proud hills gazed only at distant seas and down long vistas of time, till time itself turned a great, slow circle and brought across the plain two brothers, a child, a Clever Woman, and a girl.

The brothers rode a motorbike, shooting along

the highway like a bullet, wavering now and then because bike and riders were overloaded. They carried camping gear, an item or two of clothing, a minimum of food, and equipment for a private experiment. Terry, aged fourteen and riding pillion, believed that the experiment was private for business reasons. Lance, who was nineteen and attended university, had told him so. They swerved off the highway, onto an unpaved road that ran through heath and scrub toward the hills.

The child was still in town. He crouched in his playpen, attacking the veranda floor with a plastic hammer and chisel. His parents hurried back and forth, busily loading a small trailer, and whenever they passed he would demand the real tools they were packing. Paul would answer, "Not now," or Helen would say enticingly, "Car, Kevin," as she hurried by. At this, Kevin would smile with great charm and roll his head about, hoping to attract attention, while Paul shouted, "Where's the jerrican? We'll want water for tonight!" or Helen called, "Have you seen that other specimen box anywhere?"

The Clever Woman drove an old gray car north toward the hills, keeping to a steady fifty miles an hour; for, like the car, she was too old to register kilometers. She was going to camp for a few days under the hills, to tend the magic places of her people, for she was the last who knew how.

Her name was Mrs. Willet. The wind drew strands of gray hair from under her faded-blue headscarf and wrapped them around her brown, wrinkled cheeks; her limp, black skirt and red cardigan bulged at the waist; her feet were heavily veined above her canvas shoes. But she gripped the steering wheel firmly with fine-boned, delicate hands, raised her chin in determination to see over the hood, and aimed the car with zest at the flying highway. She did not sing but listened to a song in her head.

She had no tent but the car. Her gear was stacked on the roomy back seat or tumbled on the floor under an old, brown rug. From time to time she checked it in the rearview mirror: clothes . . . food . . . ice-cream containers . . . yellow clay and mutton fat . . . the skin bag with the ancient stones, the *booliah.* In old times, people managed without ice-cream containers and mutton fat; but those people were never alone in the haunted country, and for them time didn't count.

The lidded pan was under the billies. Sleeping bag on the floor. The mirror didn't catch it, only now when it moved. . . .

Moved?

Mrs. Willet steered onto the verge and

stopped the car. She twisted in her seat to see over the back: there was a lot too much down there. "Come out," she ordered.

The brown rug heaved and fell back. Jo Murray sat up, smiling with triumph, ready to coax or to battle, almost, but not quite, sure of her ability to manage Mrs. Willet. Jo was fourteen, fair-skinned and gray-eyed, with brown hair that the rug had teased into a bush.

Mrs. Willet gazed at her with resignation. "You're sweating," she pointed out. "All in a mess. That's dolled up, for these days, hey?"

Jo tossed her head, but this was not a moment for retort. She said, "Granny," half coaxing and half defiant.

"Better come and sit by me like a grown woman. And don't call me granny; your mother never liked it."

Jo had already slammed the rear door and opened the front. "Best granny I ever had," she declared; for she believed that Mrs. Willet did like it, and besides, her mother wasn't there.

"All the thanks I get," grumbled Mrs. Willet, restarting the motor. "Wasting time taking you home again."

"Granny!" shouted Jo. "You can't!" But she knew Mrs. Willet could, and held the door open, ready to jump. "You'll never get out to your camp before dark!"

"Shut the door," said Mrs. Willet crisply. Jo remained poised. "Shut it or we go nowhere." She switched off the ignition. "I can camp here as well as there. Shut the door."

Jo shut it but kept a grip on the handle. "You're so hard, Granny," she complained. "Is that from getting old? When I was little I really loved you, did you know that? When you took me out to the hills that other time and you used to hide me in a safe place while you were busy, it was wonderful. I thought you were special. You've never left me by myself before when Mum was on a buying trip; never once till now. What have I done? What's gone wrong?"

"I told you," said Mrs. Willet with the patience of rock. "I got things to do that it's right I should do on my own. When you were little I had no choice; you were on my hands. Now you're not my worry. Your mother never asked me, and no more she should. You're old enough to have sense."

"But that's not fair! You know Mum went in a rush! She thought you'd be right next door, like always! She just knew I'd have the sense to stay with you."

"I don't see much sense, hiding in someone's car on a trip like this when they haven't got the stuff to feed you. No shops out there, you know."

"Right!" cried Jo, hurtling about to kneel on

the seat and reach into the back. "So I brought my own! Potatoes, to roast in the fire! Baked beans—see, Granny? Cheese; have you brought that? Eggs. Bread. I've got tons, you can share it! Oh, Granny, let me come. It's lonely with the house empty and school out and everyone away."

"Some might say it's lonelier where I'm going. No shops, no discos, nothing for you. What would you do all day?"

"Get firewood, cart water, wash clothes, anything. There's always something to do in the day. It's night that's lonely. Oh, Granny, let me come."

Mrs. Willet gazed at the highway with patient, knowing eyes. They were so dark that the pupils hardly showed, and this made them seem all-seeing like the eyes of spirits. She thought it was a rare treat these days to hear the girl wheedling like the child she used to be, and no fault of hers that the mother hadn't spoken. The hills were no place to take a girl with her mother not knowing; but it wasn't right that the young should be left alone, waiting for life to hunt them out like a goanna after a possum. They needed the old to support and steady them.

"Granny? I can come, can't I?"

Brought her own grub, too—and no notion how much it took to feed a person for days. Not much notion of anything, good or bad; and you couldn't handle a girl of fourteen like you could a child of five. And there was work to do. . . .

"Granny!" roared Jo, her patience running out.

Mrs. Willet withdrew her eyes from the highway. She had not even remembered the sorrow in the hills, for that was a story lost in time.

"Now you listen to me," she said. "What I've got to do, it's real. It's not a game. It's got to be done right, the proper way. If I take you, that's got to be the proper way too: me the old woman, the one in charge; you the young one doing what she's told."

"It's always that way," said Jo indignantly.

"Never mind always. I want a promise for this time, or I'm driving home."

"Honestly, Granny, you never trust anyone. I promise."

"We'll see, then," said Mrs. Willet, starting the motor.

The gray car went on along the highway, and the hills sprang up from the plain. They held Jo's eyes, though she was restless with triumph, and restarted the song in Mrs. Willet's head.

"Will there be water out there now, Granny?"

"For those that know."

"Isn't there a place called . . . Somebody's Tank?" Jo glanced sideways. "Tricket's Tank?"

"You never saw that with me. That's off in the heath."

"How far? Maybe I once went for a walk and found it."

"With its name written up, only you couldn't read then. As if I'd let a child wander off on its own. You've got it into your head from somewhere else."

They left the highway for a scoured, sandy track between heath and stunted eucalypt. Mrs. Willet drove with careful relish while Jo bounced around in her seat.

"I remember it! It's just the same! Look, a wallaby!"

"Sure to be," said Mrs. Willet, listening to the song in her head. "Sit still, there's a good girl."

"Sorry. Oh, Granny, an emu! I swear I saw an emu!"

"You might," said Mrs. Willet. "Sit still."

"There's another track. Where does that go?"

"Tricket's Tank."

"Oh," said Jo, turning to look back. She wondered if Terry Burnett had arrived and how he could ride his bike so far and what he would say when she sprang her secret surprise.

They drove suddenly out of heath into forest, and Mrs. Willet parked the car amid trees. The marri-gums, spreading their blossom, hid the hills that loomed over them; yet the hills were present, both imminent and remote. Jo gazed into the branches, searching for them.

"Tomorrow we'll climb up there."

"We won't. Give a hand, like a good girl. Dark's coming."

"Only in the trees," Jo argued, dragging a box from the car. "It's still sunny up there."

"Dark comes fast, and there's only a torch," said Mrs. Willet from deeper in the forest. She was setting stones, collecting sticks, and breaking twigs, for a fire.

"We've got the headlamps."

"It's a long walk out, and there's no garage. We don't want to waste batteries."

"I only meant if we get bitten by a snake."

"We won't. Put those boxes in the boot; you'll want the back seat for sleeping."

"Where will you be?"

"In my old sleeping bag by the fire. I could do with more wood for it."

Jo gathered sticks, pausing and lifting her head at the sound of a motor. Mrs. Willet also lifted her head from the fire. The motor came near, stopped for a moment, and drove on past. In a little while it stopped again.

"Someone else camping," said Jo, bringing her sticks.

Mrs. Willet grunted. "I never should've brought you," she said crossly, "and your mother not knowing."

"Oh, Granny, what rubbish! *Why* shouldn't you?"

"Have sense, girl. Leaving you here on your own all day with strangers just over the ridge? It's not right."

"I have got *some* sense; I'm not a little kid. I can look after myself."

Mrs. Willet grunted again. "I'll have a look at them in the morning and we'll see. There's the billy if you want to get some water. Just up the slope a bit."

Jo took the billycan and went up the slope through the forest. It was evening here, though the treetops were gilded with sun. The slope leveled and began to dip. She followed it down into a muddy hollow and found a pool.

It lay under a high ledge of rock patched with moss and fern, at the entrance to a dark, mysterious gully. Rushes hung with creepers made a margin round the pool and speared upward through its still water. Little white swamp flowers shone here and there along the rim. Jo picked her way toward it, getting mud on her blue canvas shoes.

Crouching, she filled the billy with water. Tiny rafts of weed or slime floated in, and perhaps a wriggler or two. That might be useful. She carried it back briskly, sloshing a little on her jeans.

"Granny, this water's yuck. I don't think it's safe."

Mrs. Willet was breaking an egg into a panful of beans and gravy. "It never killed you last time," she said.

"Well . . . boiled, I suppose . . . But I'll look for good water tomorrow. It'll be something to do while you're working."

"Suit yourself, long as you don't get lost."

Jo laughed. "Lost! How could anyone get lost, with the hills standing up like God?"

"You don't want to talk like that. You might be heard."

They ate beans with eggs poached in the gravy and drank tea brewed in a small billy filled from the large one. A star or two hung between marri branches, and the cold crept silently up from the heath. Under the looming shadow of the hills the little fire flickered, lighting or hiding the faces of Jo and Mrs. Willet.

"It's a shame you can't come climbing, Granny. There must be a magical view."

"You won't see it, girl. No climbing; it's dangerous. People get killed."

"But Granny! I'm just going to see if I can climb that cliff behind the pool and get into the gully!"

"You're not going at all. You made a promise, or you'd be back in town. There's risks up there you don't know. Stay off the hills."

It was too soon for another battle. In dignified silence Jo helped with the washing up and went to bed, wrapped in a cocoon of brown rug on the back seat of the car.

She woke to a shaft of sunlight striking the top of the forest, lighting a filmy curtain of mist that hung between the trees. Bird calls were sharp and clear as dew. Everything was fresh and chill, newly made from night. Jo climbed out of the car with her sponge bag and towel. There was a pleasant smell of smoke: Mrs. Willet must be up already.

She was at the fire, stirring milk powder into hot water. She wore a man's overalls and a pink satin blouse with the red cardigan on top. Her shoes were muddy from the pool, and the billies were full.

"Isn't it lush?" shouted Jo. "Isn't it *cold*?"

"Warmer by the fire," said Mrs. Willet. "Better wash quick before the milk gets cold." She offered an ice-cream container for a washbasin.

"In that? I'd rather strip off and jump in. It's not *icy* cold, Granny!"

"Maybe. And maybe there's some don't mind drinking their bathwater. There's others mightn't like it."

Jo grinned. "That water's so yuck, nothing could make it worse." But she took the container and went on up the slope.

The pool made a very private bathroom. Jo stripped off her pajamas and, standing barefoot among the reeds, splashed and soaped and uttered sharp cries of shock. The rock ledge caught her cries and threw them back; and the sorrow that lived in the hills came drifting, frail as cobweb, down the gully to see.

Jo washed away the soap with floods of brown-flecked water, pouring it over herself with the container and shouting protests at every scoop; and the sorrow watched, yearning, and drank youth and vigor and play.

Sister! it called with longing when at last she fled, wrapped only in her towel. But Jo was running for warmth, and to shock Mrs. Willet. She did not hear.

2

JO DRESSED AS CAREFULLY AS SHE could in the back seat of the car and went running back to the fire for breakfast. Mrs. Willet's dark eyes took in the carefully teased hair and the ridiculous butterfly that bobbed above it on a wire affixed to a hidden comb. "All dolled up for the bush," she said, but with a smile in her voice.

"Why not?" said Jo. "Are you having all that toast?"

"Not me. Done long ago and ready to move." Mrs. Willet raked out the last of the fire and reached for her canvas bag. "You stay off those hills, like a good girl. That's no place to be on your own. There's mist and stones falling and I don't know what."

Jo reached for another piece of toast. "I told you: I'm going to Tricket's Tank to look for decent water."

Mrs. Willet nodded and went away east,

through the trees that were spilling the perfume of honey. She had still to visit the strange camp over the ridge. A flock of black cockatoos swept by, shrieking. Jo finished the toast and set off on the road south.

The track to Tricket's Tank ran off it, walled in by heath. Bright green parrots, with a touch of vivid red on their black heads, cried *twenty-eight! twenty-eight!* as they tore at the blossoms of stunted marri trees. There were heath flowers hiding from the autumn and pink everlastings lifting their heads. The butterfly bobbed above Jo's hair. She reached a patch of taller, greener scrub rising above the heath. She knew this must be Tricket's Tank and left the road and crept into the scrub through heath. She wanted to appear, not to arrive.

Peeping through a screen of hakea, she could see a fireplace cluttered with plates, mugs, a backpack, and a sweater, and, farther off, a small tent beside a pool. Someone came out of the tent: Terry himself, with his long, thin face and his hair that was almost white. He was taking a billy to fill at the pool. When he straightened and turned, Jo was standing at the tent.

"Hi," she said, very casually. Terry Burnett dropped the billy, splashing his jeans and flooding his canvas shoes, and Jo laughed and laughed.

"Jo Murray!" shouted Terry. "What are you doing here?"

"Just passing. Did you think it was the fuzz?"

"It wouldn't matter. How did you get here?"

"Walked," said Jo carelessly. "Thought I'd have a look at the great experiment." It was much too soon to explain away her surprise. She was still smiling innocently when the surprise turned around and struck back.

Out of the tent came a stranger, a tall young man in a black windbreaker. "Well, now," he said, eyeing Jo from head to foot and staring with appreciation at the butterfly. "Who's this? Introduce me, mate."

"It's Jo Murray," said Terry lamely. "She's in my year at school. She just dropped in." To Jo he added, "It's my brother, Lance. He's at university." He glowered at Lance.

"Oh," said Jo flatly. She was never going to speak to Terry Burnett again. There hadn't been a word about his university brother.

Now she had to explain how she happened, by accident, to be staying with Granny Willet, and how she had come looking for water because theirs was yuck; and Terry had to explain that he and Lance were growing gold-top mushrooms because Lance knew people who would buy them and Lance said it was legal. Lance listened, smiling as if he didn't believe them. It made Jo prickly. "Why is it legal?" she demanded. "I didn't think any drugs were legal."

"They can't stop natural mushrooms, can they?" argued Terry politely. "They'd have to arrest Australia."

"Oh. Well . . . Sorry I butted in. I'll get back."

But at last Lance was smiling properly. "Rubbish," he said. "We don't have many good-looking visitors. Stay for lunch and we'll run you back on the motorbike. Eh, mate?"

"Right on," said Terry with relief.

"Oh!" said Jo on a new note, smiling back. She had never ridden on a motorbike.

Terry took her to see the experiment: four plastic trays filled with earth. Looking at them, Jo said accusingly, "You never let on about your brother. You made a fool of me."

"Have sense! How did I know you'd turn up out here?"

"If it's all so legal, why don't you do it at home?"

"Lance says the customers'd want too much of the action."

"Maybe they do," Jo retorted. "Listen: more visitors."

They had not noticed the sound of a motor until now, when it was near. Lance's head was thrust into the tent. "Throw a towel over those trays. Someone's coming."

Terry draped the trays in towels, and he and Jo went back to the fireplace. Round a bend of the track, between walls of heath, a four-wheel-drive appeared and came on to the camp. There it stopped.

"Sorry," said Paul Macgregor from the driver's seat. "I see you're ahead of us. We'll leave you to it."

They all gazed dumbly back until Helen explained.

"It was just the water. Ours is a dry camp. But this is a bit too far for us anyway."

"Oh!" cried Jo, suddenly understanding. "You're camping near us, aren't you? You came in last night, about sunset. You can share our water; it's all right if you boil it."

Helen smiled, gripping Kevin, who was trying to stand on the seat. "We know your water, we camped there last time. But we thought we'd try not to intrude. You must be Jo. We met Mrs. Willet this morning."

"She thought you might be dangerous criminals. Is that your little boy? Isn't he lush?"

Helen laughed. "Kevin? Lush?"

"He's a disaster," said Paul. "We'll get no work done, but we can't help it. His grandmother's away, so we have no baby-sitter." Kevin smiled widely at everyone and buried his face on his mother's shoulder.

"I can baby-sit for you," Jo offered. "Tomorrow, anyway." She introduced Lance and Terry, and Lance asked polite questions about geology; he had seen Paul and Helen at the university. Then the Macgregors said good-bye and drove away.

Lance relaxed. "Grub's up," he said.

They ate sardine sandwiches washed down with fruit juice, and discussed the problem of transporting a whole camp, with equipment for an experiment, in two backpacks on one motorbike. Jo was shocked to find that the boys had brought very little food and no potatoes.

"Too heavy," said Terry.

"You can have some of mine," said Jo, and told how she had defeated Mrs. Willet by bringing her own food and hiding under the rug. Although he was a university man, Lance laughed louder than Terry. This led Jo into acting a quick sketch of Mrs. Willet declining to drink Jo's bathwater. She was good at impromptu sketches, and Lance laughed again.

Afterward he brought the motorbike from behind the tent and straddled it while Terry showed Jo how to mount the pillion and where to put her feet. Terry sat in front on the fuel tank, with his feet spread wide.

"We can only get away with this in the bush or the back yard," said Lance, kicking the engine till it roared. Jo clung to him with fingers of iron; the bike moved, swayed and straightened. Lance rode and Terry steered.

They came bumping up from heath into forest and stopped by the old gray car. The boys admired it while Jo rooted in its trunk. She tipped most of her potatoes into Granny's groceries, leaving only a few in the bag. To those she added a can of something called Hotpot. "You can't carry eggs on that thing, can you?" she asked, pondering.

"Terry can," said Lance, gazing upward. "Have you been on the hills yet?"

"Granny has a fit if you even talk about it. She says it's dangerous."

"She would, I suppose, with you here by yourself. A bit different now, with three of us."

"She did say on my own," said Jo, wrapping eggs in paper towels. She tucked them carefully into the bag and handed it to Terry, who propped it by the wheel of the bike.

"Right," said Lance. "We'll just go up a bit and have a look." He started up the slope, and the others followed.

A wide gully-mouth below the pool invited them in. It steepened almost at once, and they helped themselves up its side by gripping trees and vines. Soon they were scrambling from ledge to ledge, looking down into the gully or up to great haunches of rock, withdrawn and still. Jo was glad she was not alone. It did seem dangerous, and it felt like they were climbing up some great monster, alive and savage but asleep.

"I don't think we should go too far," she ventured. "We still have to get back."

"Not this way," said Lance from above. "We're climbing the side of a ridge. We'll get up there and walk down the ridge. Easy."

They climbed on, for by now they could do nothing else. Lance shouted a warning as a stone gave under his foot and came crashing down. Terry's hand was bleeding from thorns, and Jo had to keep stopping to untangle her butterfly. Then Lance gave a muffled shout and wriggled out of sight: they had reached the ridge.

It was only an outstretched paw of the monster hills, but it held them above the plain like eagles. Far away to the south lay the misty hills of the coast. To left and right, massive rock faces and tree-hung slopes crowded above steep, shadowed gullies. Far above, visible at last, those high cliffs loomed into the sunlit sky. Jo greeted them with a shout of triumph: "Hi, there!"

And the cliffs or the hills or the dark places shouted back: *Hi, there. . . . Hi, there. . . . Hi, there. . . . Hi, there. . . .*

It was startling, for the answers rang from all around, loud and near or faint and far away, running to and fro in the hills, separating and mingling. Jo was astonished. Lance and Terry, gazing over the plains, swung round and laughed.

Jo shouted again, making it into a game: "Where are you?"

This time the echoes, crossing and mingling, tangled her words. *Where are you? . . . Where? . . . Are you there? . . . Are you? . . . Where are you?* The calls seemed to run about in search of her, and Jo caught her breath.

"Come over here!" called Terry, taking his turn. The echo answered teasingly. *Come over! . . . Come here . . . over here! . . . Come over, come! . . . Here, over here!*

"No! You come!" shouted Lance, and the echo played with the pause as well as the words.

No! You! . . . No, come! . . . You come! . . . No! . . . You! . . . Come, you come! . . . No!

"Look," said Jo suddenly, "the sun's gone. It gets dark so quickly. Let's go."

"It's only the ridge casting a shadow," said Lance kindly. "Look at all the sun out there."

"You look," she retorted. "Down there, where we have to go, there'll be no more sun till morning."

Terry agreed. "Better start. But I'm glad we made it." He shouted good-bye to the echo as Lance started down the ridge.

Good-bye! . . . Good-bye! . . . Good-bye! . . . Good-bye! called the cliffs and the hills and the dark places.

"*Why* does it do that?" said Jo crossly, grabbing at a shrub to keep from running down the slope onto Lance.

"It's an echo, isn't it?" he said, looking back.

"I know. But when I shouted it sounded like me."

"Of course it did. It's the same sound bouncing back."

"So why didn't it sound like you and Terry? When you shouted, why did it still sound like me?"

Lance considered briefly. "It didn't. You imagined it."

She had no time to argue, for the ridge was too steep and stony. When she let it hurry her, she bumped into Lance; when she paused, Lance vanished and Terry ran into her.

"We're being followed," he panted, looking backward. The upper ridge was lost in a sudden fog. It went rolling over the edge into the gully and sent misty trailers curling down the ridge. It was hard to believe it could have come so fast.

They went on, running and stumbling down the steepest parts and steadying themselves when they could. The mist seemed to drift quite slowly; but it overtook them, touching them with light, damp fingers as it flowed past. In the white dimness they found themselves among mist-softened shapes of tall trees and knew they were near the camp. Jo bumped into Lance again: he had stopped and was peering ahead. Someone was coming, toiling up the slope. Mist dimmed the red cardigan, but Jo saw it and muttered something cross.

Aloud she called gaily, "Granny! You're early! Are you finished already? Look what I found at Tricket's Tank!"

Mrs. Willet stood gazing up through the mist. "You're all right, then," she said, and turned abruptly away down the slope. It was clear that she was upset. Jo ran after her.

"It's Terry and Lance Burnett, Granny," she explained, while the boys hung back awkwardly. Mrs. Willet gave no sign of hearing. "Terry's in my class, I know him quite well. And there they were, at Tricket's Tank, doing a botany project!" Mrs. Willet strode on, ignoring her. "So they brought me home. And there were three of us, so we came up here."

Mrs. Willet turned suddenly down the side of the ridge. They all followed, the boys hiding grins and Jo with angry little jerks of the head. It was embarrassing to be treated like a naughty child in front of her friends, especially in front of a university man.

The car and the motorbike appeared through the mist, and Mrs. Willet went striding past. Jo stayed defiantly to see the boys mount, Terry, on the pillion, nursing the plastic bag. Then she marched on to the camp, arriving with a flounce.

Mrs. Willet chose not to see. She was feeding a new fire with sticks.

"I think," said Jo in a high, tight voice, "you were *very rude* to the Burnett boys."

Mrs. Willet grunted, placing sticks. "They won't mind. They got our spuds and stuff, didn't they?"

"Mine! I only gave them mine! When they'd given me lunch, and they hardly had anything!"

"You must've ate a big lunch," said Mrs. Willet. "So now we're short. Doesn't matter, the way it turns out." She looked up at last, with her dark eyes that seemed to have no pupils. "I'll be taking you home tomorrow, and your tucker-bag with you."

This was a shock that Jo covered as well as she could. "Don't trouble! Lance and Terry will take me when I'm ready. I never knew you were so mean, Granny Willet. All this fuss over a few potatoes and eggs!"

"Not for that," said Mrs. Willet.

"Why, then?"

"Because I can't trust you, that's why. Scheming and telling lies so you could come out here with your fancy friends—making a fool of me. Had a good laugh at old Granny Willet, didn't you?"

This was so nearly true that Jo turned red. She didn't know why she fought so often with Granny these days, but she hadn't meant to make a fool of her. It was just a joke that had turned into a mess. She stood in a red-faced, sulky silence.

"I'll allow I should've known," said Mrs. Willet. "I've known you long enough. But you made me a promise, my girl, not to go in those hills. If I can't trust your promise—"

"But I didn't!" cried Jo. "You're not fair! You said not on my own, and I didn't! I wouldn't even go with Terry; he's too young. But Lance is at *university,* Granny, he's *quite mature,* and there were *three* of us! That's not on my own!"

Mrs. Willet placed more sticks on the fire. She knew she was too angry, but she was shaken by shock and a fear she could not believe. Maybe she should never have brought the girl— But here she was and, true enough, she couldn't be packed home. She was on Mrs. Willet's hands; and now these brothers . . . But fear could make more fools than any bit of a girl could do, and it was no good losing tempers.

She said, "We can sort that out: I'll allow I might've said on your own, but it's not what I meant. I don't want you in those hills scaring the daylights out of me. Not on your own. Not with your friends. Not at all. Long as you're here, there's got to be a promise I can trust. Right?"

"Right," said Jo, sulky but relieved, and she slumped down by the fire. She watched Mrs. Willet begin mixing the dough for a damper to be baked in the pan. After a minute she said guiltily, "Are we really short of food?"

"We'll get by," said Mrs. Willet, and changed the subject. "These others over the ridge seem like good people. Got a little boy. They'll be wanting water."

"I know. The little boy's Kevin. I'm baby-sitting him tomorrow. Granny, why did you go up the ridge? I mean, with all these hills, how did you know where to go?"

"Fetch the butter, like a good girl. For all you know, I was hunting you for hours."

"Were you?"

"No." The night had closed round the fire. Mrs. Willet groped for plates and knives, taking time to relax her breathing and loosen the muscles of her throat; refusing to be shaken by fear. "I heard you, girl," she said.

"The motorbike, I suppose."

"It never went up there. I heard the calling."

"Oh, Granny, and you thought something was wrong—I was calling for help! I'm sorry."

Mrs. Willet lifted the pan from the fire and broke the damper into pieces. "Never mind," she said. "That's over. Now it's time for dinner."

Later, in her sleeping bag, it was time to think. The fire was a red glow under gray ash; the night stood over it, profound and aware, breathing like the hills. Mrs. Willet did not refuse fear but faced it in the way of her people.

She remembered old stories not thought of since she was a girl, and how they might lie in the mind and twist its thinking. She thought of the child in the camp across the ridge: he too fitted the pattern. No good warning people like that, and surely no need. For them, the sun rose in the morning because of Kevin; they would have him near.

She considered tomorrow's baby-sitting: a good thing, best for both, as long as the girl was safe here in camp before the dangerous time of night. Best if Mrs. Willet herself got home while the sun was in the sky.

She thought of these brothers, whatever their name was, and wished them far away. No good talking to them, either; no good talking to anyone. And at that, fear took hold of her again and she was suddenly, bitterly lonely.

She longed for the people who were gone, who would listen and understand; the people who knew what it might be that ran about in the hills calling for Jo. And while she longed for them the fire died; the sorrow in the hills could watch it no longer, and drifted off to high and lonely places.

3

JO SLEPT TILL SUNLIGHT MADE A DAZzle on the car windows, and woke to find Mrs. Willet already gone. The fire had fallen apart into warm ash and hot charcoal, but the tea was still hot. The old iron pan held Jo's breakfast, its lid a protection from ants.

It was good to feel alone and free, as if she were in charge of the camp. Perhaps she would wash yesterday's shirt and underclothes, or sunbathe, or explore the forest. Not visit Tricket's Tank again, anyhow; not today, after Granny's being so upset. She bathed at the pool, dressed, and had breakfast. After that she suddenly remembered the Macgregors and Kevin.

How awful! They must have been working for hours! They would think she made promises she didn't mean to keep. Jo leaped up and began to run.

It was not far, only around the foot of a ridge and into the next gully. She found the four-wheel-drive and a small trailer, and a clothesline rigged between two trees with some of Kevin's things drying. She stood and listened. There were clinking sounds quite near, probably of tools on rock, and one angry yell from Kevin. She followed the sounds.

Paul and Helen Macgregor were a little way up a rise, chipping gently at a rock face. Below squatted Kevin with a hammer, earnestly aiming at a stone and sometimes hitting it. They all looked up in surprise when Jo shouted and waved.

"I'm sorry—I slept in!" she said when she was near. "Granny must have gone off early."

Helen seemed a little worried. "My dear, you can't really give up your holiday to mind this demon."

"Why not? I'm not doing anything else today."

"He has problems just now: he's fixated on tools and his parents. It's quite common at this age, but no fun for baby-sitters. He'll be a pest."

Jo laughed. "Don't worry, we'll have fun." She had never been a baby-sitter before, but lots of her friends did it, and anyone could see that Kevin was sweet.

He greeted her with a wide, warm smile, said something incomprehensible, and aimed a blow at the stone. After that he ignored Jo when he could, and uttered short, angry yells when he could not. This irritated Paul, depressed Helen, and made Jo feel clumsy and useless. At last she seized Kevin, hammer and all, and carried him struggling and yelling down the gully. She was trying to interest him in bigger and better stones, and Kevin was aiming hammer blows at her instead, when Helen arrived to say it was time for lunch.

"He has a sleep after lunch," said Helen, while they ate chicken sandwiches in the trailer. "I don't think you can wait around for that. You've been kind enough already."

"Oh, no!" cried Jo, anxious to improve her baby-sitting image. "I *can* help with that. You put him off to sleep and go back to work, and I'll wait till he wakes. Then I can bring him up to you."

"Fine," said Helen doubtfully. "He does sleep like a log, as long as he has his old blanket."

Settled into a bunk by his mother, Kevin did fall instantly and deeply asleep. Jo felt useful again; it was peaceful but boring. She sat on the trailer steps, waiting for him to wake and listening to the distant clink of tools. Then came a more interesting sound: the growl of a motorbike coming near.

Terry and Lance! Coming to look for her? But they'd miss her, and she was so near! It would be mean not to see them and explain. She saw that

Kevin was still profoundly asleep and crept away from the trailer.

It was Lance alone. He had come to take her for a ride on the bike, to make up for yesterday's trouble. Deeply disappointed, Jo explained about the baby-sitting.

"That's bad," said Lance. "But we could burn along the track a bit till the kid wakes up. If it's so near, you can take a look between rides. Suit yourself."

"Of course I can," said Jo quickly. If Kevin woke, fixated as he was, he'd go straight to his parents and they'd think Jo was awful. But it was hard to offend anyone as grand as Lance, and Kevin was too deeply asleep to wake yet.

Nothing warned her that Kevin, waking as easily as he slept and climbing down the trailer steps with his old knitted blanket, might go anywhere: toward the chink of his parents' tools, after the roar of the motorbike, down into the heath, or up into the hills.

Mrs. Willet had left camp in the gray dawn, to be sure of coming back while the sun was in the sky. Her mind was at ease about the baby-sitting; she needed only to be sure the girl was home before night.

During the day her work left no room for fear, filling her mind with secrets and wonder. The secrets were hidden with a cunning that was deep and sly and devious, for they hid themselves. They were ordinary things that lay in the open for anyone to see: one tree in a forest, one stone on a hillside, a grassy hollow, a pool. It was only their truth that was secret, and only those who knew it could find them. That was the wonder.

One stone among many, stroked to a polish by thousands of hands and tingling to the touch; one pool closing silently over the gift of leaves; one hollow where tentative grass hid the ancient tracks: No one without teaching could tell that these were the sacred storehouses of life. No one could know that the stone held the spirits of unborn children, and would give them up when the right hands stroked it and the right person sang the proper song. No one could see that the pool held the spirits of food plants, or that wallabies were born when the right feet danced through the hollow. Only when you knew them could you feel them waiting, open and innocent, secretive, wary and alive.

They waited for service by the elders; now, in an empty country, they waited for a lost people, and only Mrs. Willet came. But she came wearing on her dark face the pattern that showed her right and her reverence, a pattern painted in clay blended with fat; and she offered her service with the proper respect.

"Don't be angry with me, now. I'm only a woman, but I'm old. You don't want to hurt me, I'm all there is." Then she gave each its service, in song or touch or symbol, or in the enigmatic patterns of the booliah stones. The secret things accepted her for her age and wisdom, and in return they gave her peace.

They kept her at peace while she trudged home in the sunlight, past the Macgregors' camp under the ridge, and heard Paul's voice shouting, "Kevin!" It didn't trouble her. Songs and spells blew around her like a willy-willy, while her spirit lay in stillness at the center.

She rounded the end of the separating ridge and turned in toward her own camp. There was the gray car, farther on among trees; that motorbike was near it again. Mrs. Willet's spirit grew restless.

Then Jo's voice shouted, shrill and anxious: "Kevin! Where are you? Kevin!"

And the fear stirred again. For the hills answered softly and teasingly, in voices full of mischief that went running to and fro: *Kevin! Where are you? Kevin! Kevin! Kevin!*

Mrs. Willet fought down a weakness in her knees and went faster. "Old fool," she told herself angrily; for in all her questioning fear she had never thought of the motorbike or of how easily it might lure Jo away from the little boy.

There was no one at the camp. She went on toward the pool and met Jo coming from it with the tall, dark youth. He was frowning. Jo's face was white and dazed. When she saw Mrs. Willet she ran.

"Oh, Granny! Kevin's gone! What will I do? He was sound asleep, I only left for a minute, he *couldn't* get far, he couldn't! But we can't find him. What will I do?"

"Kevin!" shouted Paul's voice distantly from beyond the eastern ridge; and now Mrs. Willet heard its tension. And down a gully, from out of the hills, the answers came ringing and running. *Kevin! Kevin! Kevin!* They were not the echoes of Paul's tight voice. They called lightly and playfully, like a teasing girl.

Mrs. Willet wasted no words. To Jo's pleading question and her white, drawn face she answered, "You'll come with me," and turned to the youth. "Lance. That's your name? You go and help the parents. Or get the police. Don't stop here." She swung back to Jo. "Fetch the old brown rug out of the car. Quick, now! Bring it here."

Jo flew down the slope, and Mrs. Willet faced and outfaced fear. It was still a fear she could not believe—but it was there, and it must be dealt with.

She went on to look at the pool, since that must always be done when a child is lost. There was no sign; she had not expected any. The ledge beyond the pool was both high and sheer enough to bar a two-year-old from the gully behind. The eastern ridge was steep and broken. Small children were surprising, but if Kevin did climb it he would come nearer his own camp, where his parents were calling. To the west, another, smaller gully ran up between two spurs from the main ridge. Mrs. Willet went back to meet Jo.

Jo came stumbling and panting, clutching the old rug. There were tears on her face; no time for those now. Mrs. Willet folded the rug small and tucked it back under Jo's arm. "Why did you come this way?"

"The pool," sniffed Jo. "They got water this morning. He might remember."

"He might, but he's not there. Come on, now." Mrs. Willet headed for the smaller gully, and Jo stumbled after her.

"Do you think—?"

"I don't know. We'll look."

The gully mouth opened wide, full of channeled and waterworn rock. Jo remembered crossing it with Lance and Terry to climb its southern wall, but Mrs. Willet took the northern side. There, amid vines swinging down from above, a faint track climbed up and down along a narrow ledge. Mrs. Willet mounted it with a plodding sureness of foot, and Jo followed blindly. It climbed higher, leading them above the narrowing, boulder-strewn floor of the gully.

"Watch how we go," said Mrs. Willet over her shoulder, stepping carefully over a gap in the ledge. "You might have to come back on your own."

"Why, Granny?" cried Jo in alarm.

"Don't panic, girl. Watch." But in a moment Mrs. Willet explained: "If we find the boy, you might have to take him down fast. I might have to wait. I'm slower."

Jo lifted a white face to the green and darkening gloom between frightening walls of rock, to the hills mounting above like monsters and the sunny sky so very far above. Somewhere there was a sound of water dripping. She could not believe they would find Kevin here; but if they did, she thought sickly, he was sure to be hurt. He would need to be taken down fast. And while she thought this, Mrs. Willet stooped to pounce on something.

It was Kevin's old knitted blanket.

Jo stared at it. That little boy, so soundly asleep: How could he have wakened so quickly and carried his blanket all this way, climbing along this broken ledge? Full of horror and hope she gave a desperate shout: "Kevin!"

And from all around and very near the echoes came back, laughing, teasing, coaxing, crooning: *Kevin! Kevin! Kevin! Kevin!*

Mrs. Willet had seized Jo round the shoulders and was pressing the knitted blanket against her face. "Shush!" she whispered. "Don't shout. Don't shout." She took the blanket away and gave the girl a little shake that was partly a hug. "Keep quiet. Stay by me. Watch. Look for mist."

Jo gasped. She was shivering, yet it was a gasp of crazy laughter. Nothing was real anymore. "Mist! That was yesterday! I'm looking for Kevin—it's his blanket."

"I know." The dark eyes searched her face. "You're needed: Act like a woman." Mrs. Willet released her and turned away, twisting the knitted blanket round her own arm. She went ahead, stopping often to examine the rocks in front, and above, and below.

Jo followed, searching too; clinging to rocks and vines, sometimes slipping, sometimes sobbing a little. The sky was still very far above, a narrow slice between the walls of rock. When they had gone slowly on for another five minutes Mrs. Willet paused, gazing ahead and to the right.

Jo saw that there was a place where the rock

wall curved inward, a shallow cave behind a boulder. Something moved there: Jo, her nerves stretched, made a little sound. But the movement was only a drifting wisp of mist.

Mrs. Willet reached behind and gripped her arm. "Keep behind me. Don't come till I say," she whispered; and, still holding the knitted blanket, she moved a few steps forward. Very softly she began to call, but not to Kevin. The calling was low and gentle, almost like singing.

"Balyet! Balyet!" Granny Willet called. "You see me, Balyet, I'm here. I'm your skin, your sister."

Jo, listening, was suddenly filled with a colder sort of fear. There was nothing here, no sign of life; Granny Willet was calling to nothing. Nothing answered. Nothing could. There was only the movement of mist.

"I see you, Balyet," called Granny Willet softly. "It's daylight still, I see you by your shadow." She took a single step. "Don't be scared. I'm old, but I can't help it. I'm not like you, I have to get old." She took another step. The trail of mist wavered as if she had stirred it, and the old woman froze and was still. And Jo, sick with guilt and fear and with the memory of Paul's and Helen's shocked faces, knew this was a useless waste of time. She knew that Granny Willet was mad.

"Poor little sister. Poor girl," crooned Granny Willet, stealing another step. "He's not your boy, Balyet. They won't let you have him, you know that."

Still nothing answered. There was only a small sobbing of wind among rocks. Granny Willet crept another step, still speaking low and gentle.

"He's not your boy and he's not from your people. He's a different sort of skin. That's a stranger you've got there, Balyet."

The pale mist wavered like a shadow. The echo rang soft and confused out of the very cave, picking up a word here and there: *Stranger. . . . Boy. . . . Poor Balyet. . . .* and then, in great distress, the echo of an earlier cry: *Kevin! Kevin! Kevin!*

Jo shivered, feeling sick and cold. The massive, rocky hills seemed to close in on her, and Mrs. Willet began to sing. This, too, was chilling, for there seemed to be no music in the singing and the words were not words that Jo had ever heard. It was just a singing sound that Granny Willet was making, drifting slowly down a scale, rising and drifting down again like the wind.

As she sang, the old woman went slowly forward and the wavering mist drew back, little by little, until at last the singer stood within the cave. Still singing, she bent suddenly and was hidden by the boulder. When she stood up, she was holding Kevin wrapped in the knitted blanket.

Seeing him, Jo went stumbling forward.

"Quick. The rug," muttered Mrs. Willet, and went on singing her wind-blowing song and watching the pale mist. Kevin's eyes were closed; he was white and cold. Jo, bundling the rug around him, found that she was carrying him and being pushed away. "Go," mumbled Mrs. Willet, and sang on.

Jo never knew how she managed to get down the ledge. The limp weight in the brown rug was sometimes on her shoulder and sometimes in her arms; there were stones that rolled and vines that blinded her. There was a sharp, anxious fear for the little boy inside the rug, and a great, sobbing dread of whatever was behind. Not the wisp of mist or the singing of Granny Willet; those small, crazy things had faded from her mind the moment she saw Kevin. What followed her down the ledge was a sound, a dreadful sound.

It might have been a wild wind howling through the gullies and wailing around columns of rock, if wind could cry with hopeless agony; yet it could not be wind, for no leaf moved and no branch stirred. The air was still, yet a windy howling cried from rock to rock and came sobbing down the ledge after Jo. It drove her on, as if pain and despair were crying after her along the gully.

It fell behind as she passed into tall forest and forced herself on toward the gray car, where at last she could lay Kevin on the seat and jam down the button of the horn.

4

IT WAS DUSK WHEN MRS. WILLET CAME slowly down the slope through the marri trees. She had taken her time, for she was weary with shock and disaster narrowly averted, and with pity. She had heard the rumble of motors some time ago, but she would have known in any case that the Macgregors and Lance had gone. The forest was heavily still, undisturbed and deeply engrossed in its growing. Only Jo sat by the dead fire, slumped forward with her head on her knees.

Watching her from the forest, Mrs. Willet was filled with fresh pity. It was hard for the young—all new-painted to be grown-up, wanting to take charge, fighting off their old people—to come suddenly upon their own young weakness. It didn't used to be so hard; there was more help, once. Well, the girl must be gotten back to town before anything worse happened; at least that ought to be easy, shaken up as she was. Mrs.

Willet gathered sticks, and as soon as she reached the camp began to light the fire.

She set one or two cans near the flames, to heat for a meal later on, and made tea in the billy as soon as the water had boiled. When the tea had drawn she poured it into mugs and handed one to Jo. By now the fire had made its safe, warm circle in the night, and Jo had raised her head to watch it. She looked at Mrs. Willet in a startled way, dropped her eyes defensively, and accepted the mug of tea.

"They've gone, then," said the old woman quietly. "How was the boy?"

Jo tried to answer, failed, and tried again. "Breathing," she said, and drank.

"Wrapped him up warm, did they?" Jo nodded. "Well, then. If he was breathing, he'll be all right."

"He never opened his eyes!" cried Jo. "He was so white! He was so cold!" She had dropped her mug, and tea ran hissing into the hot ashes.

Mrs. Willet reached for the mug, refilled it, and added sugar. "You drink that," she said, offering it again. "If the boy was still breathing he'll be all right. You made good time down that ledge; I heard the horn. That was sense, blowing the horn."

Jo took the mug for the second time, stood it carefully on the ground, and began to sob.

Mrs. Willet set her own mug down and rose tiredly. She rummaged in her bundle of clothing, dragged out a woolen shawl, and wrapped it around Jo's shoulders. "Upset, were they?" she said with sympathy. "There, now. He was their boy, he was on their hands. You got on all right; you know more than you did, that's all. Drink your tea. I thought that boy—Lance, is it? I thought he might've stayed with you."

"What for?" sobbed Jo. "Anyhow, he couldn't. Terry didn't know where he was." She shook her head in a determined way, wiped her face on the ends of the shawl, and drank tea.

Mrs. Willet let time pass, now and then turning the cans at the fire. After a time she said comfortably, "We'll go home tomorrow."

Jo stared at her, startled and wary, "Why? It's only been two days. Have you finished already?"

"Near enough. I can come back later. You'll want to know how the boy is."

"I can't!" cried Jo. "I can't see them; I can't go near! No, Granny, no—let me stay!"

"That's not sense, girl. It'll ease your mind." Seeing Jo's face, she added quickly, "We'll think about it tomorrow. Fetch a couple of plates, like a good girl."

Jo made an almost physical effort to put out of her mind the faces of Paul and Helen: tense, strained, saying almost nothing, accusing her only with their eyes; and of Kevin, so white that the blue veins showed. She found the plates and turned back clutching them. "Granny," she said, "what was that awful noise? You know: that awful crying. What was it?"

Mrs. Willet had already considered such answers as dingoes or wind, but they were useless. She answered quite simply, "That? That was Balyet, poor thing."

"Bal-yet," Jo repeated. She remembered the name and added cautiously, "That's the one you were singing to, when you found Kevin."

Mrs. Willet nodded. "Aren't you going to give me those plates?" She reached out and took them.

"You said it was your sister, but you were scared. What's this . . . Bal-yet?"

"It's the language: Balyet means echo, that's all. Here's your dinner." She set one of the plates near Jo's feet.

"I'm not a little kid, Granny," said Jo, ignoring the plate. "You don't talk to echoes and sing songs to them. They don't keep their own voices and come howling after you like that. What was it? Some sort of ghost?"

"Something like that."

"And is this ghost supposed to have taken Kevin out of the caravan and carted him all the way up there? What for?"

"Not taken; he'd have wandered off, like you thought. She just coaxed him on with her calling. She's lonely, poor thing. Young like you, lived in a camp full of people; people round her all the time, and now they're gone. She wants a child or a friend to love, that's all."

"She didn't love me," grumbled Jo. "Crying around me like that." She wanted to claim that the ghost was only an echo—but Granny had already said so and Jo had ruled it out. She wanted to declare her shocked disbelief in the wavering shred of mist, and Granny's talking and singing on the ledge—but how could she, when they had brought Kevin back? She only said, knowing it was foolish, "Why did she have to do that?"

Mrs. Willet looked at her with eyes as dark as a paperbark swamp. "You were taking the boy away, weren't you? Sit down and eat. I'd never have put you through it, only we had to get the boy. You're the last one I'd have chosen. Let it go for now, and eat your dinner and get some sleep. You had a bad day. We'll talk about it tomorrow."

Jo flopped down by the fire and began to eat scorched goulash. Once she said, "That's why you didn't want me in the hills." In a little while she laid her head on her knees and drifted into an exhausted doze, until at last Mrs. Willet sent her off to bed in the car.

In the morning she was pale, heavy-eyed, and still silent. Mrs. Willet watched and said nothing; she, like Jo, had lain awake for most of the night. After breakfast she spoke casually, as if she and Jo were already agreed.

"Well, then. Better start packing if we're going home."

Jo's head jerked up, and she answered politely but quickly. "You go, Granny, if you want to. I'll stay and go home with Lance; he won't mind two trips."

It was a rehearsed answer, and Mrs. Willet's heart sank; but, leaning forward to rake out the coals, she spoke as calmly as ever. "You won't fit all your gear on that bike. I brought you, I'll take you home. That's the proper way."

"I'm not going home early because of some old ghost," said Jo forcefully. "I'm sorry if it's your sister, Granny, but still— Ghosts aren't anything. I mean, even if they're there, even if they howl, they aren't anything."

So she'd worked that out for herself, thought Mrs. Willet; Jo's real trouble was the boy, and she needed time for that. The old woman said, "I'll get in one more day, then, and we'll talk tonight."

She too had thought about things. The camp was safe; to stay on guard there would only drive the girl away from it. Better to go about her work and draw quiet out of that, coming back early as she had yesterday. She said, "Mind, I've got your promise. I count on that."

Jo only said, "I don't want to break my leg, thanks." Mrs. Willet took up her carryall, but she did not yet stride off down the slope. She stood fingering the handle of the bag.

"These friends of yours," she said. "These brothers: Lance and Terry, is it? Don't bring them here, love." Jo stiffened. "Don't get me wrong, now—go and spend the day with them if you like, have a ride on that bike, do whatever you want, you've got sense enough—only don't bring them here, like a good girl. It's not safe."

"Safe!" cried Jo hotly, firing up in defense of her friends. "I don't know what you're talking about! *What* isn't safe?"

"Nothing to do with you or them. Put it onto poor old Granny, scared of a ghost. I never should've brought you, only you promised. So now, don't bring those brothers here."

"Why don't you go home, then? If you're so scared, and you can't trust me?"

Mrs. Willet gazed at her with dark spirit-eyes. "You know why. Like you knew last night. You know I can't go and leave you. I'll go on, and we'll talk about it later." She turned and went off through the trees.

Jo sat scowling at the dead fire, letting herself feel angry and hiding inside the anger. Old people were all the same: Granny was set against Lance and Terry. And Jo wasn't even going to Tricket's Tank, as it happened. For one thing, she felt too tired to walk all that way; for another, she didn't want to talk. Not about Kevin, or Paul and Helen, or the singing and the ghost—not about anything.

She wandered about the camp, too restless to relax, wishing for some small, unimportant thing to do: a book to read, if only she'd brought one. Panties and bras to wash, then? A boring idea; and she'd have to wash them in the pool, and they'd come out brown and muddy. . . . But nothing more interesting would come into her mind, and after a lunch of banana and cheese she collected her few things and took them, with her soap, to the pool.

It was hard to know how to attack the job: If she knelt in the mud, she would probably ruin her jeans as well as her washing. Easier to stand in the water— She remembered Granny and the bathwater, but Lance had said the water was running, part of an underground river. Jo stripped off her shirt and jeans. In her underclothes, hugging her washing and the soap, she stepped down into the pool.

Her feet sank into deep ooze, and mud and brown fragments welled up around her legs. The water did not reach her knees; it was chill from the underground. Whatever sun might reach it had now passed; it lay in the shade of the forest, with a frail wisp of mist hanging in the gully above.

Jo went farther out, feeling her way with her toes while the reeds scratched her legs, until the chilly, silken water reached her waist. The shock of it broke through her depression and made her feel alive again. With mysterious things tickling at her skin, she doused her small bundle of washing, anchored bits of it here and there in the reeds, and began to soap them.

It was hard not to lose them in the water; especially when the mud squelched between her toes, or unexpected things brushed her legs and made her giggle. She was too occupied even to hear the motorbike, and did not raise her head until Terry called from the edge of the pool. Then she jumped and dropped the soap.

"You've got a cheek, Terry Burnett!" she shouted. "Can't you see I'm not dressed? Clear out!"

"Why?" asked Terry. "You look the same as on the beach. I've come to see if you're all right after yesterday."

"So now you've seen. Thanks for coming, but I don't want to talk about it."

"Is the kid all right?"

Jo winced. "How would I know? Lance saw him. Didn't he tell you?"

"Lance," said Terry darkly. "He's got a nerve, carting you off like that and making all this hoo-ha. He should've had more sense. I told Lance he's got it wrong. It's his experiment, he should stay home and water it. You're my friend, I should come round and see if you're all right."

This was interesting, and Jo laughed a little. "Lance is very nice," she said primly, rolling her wet laundry into a ball and hurling it ashore among the bushes. "It's natural for him to go ahead and do things; he's older. Besides, he's your brother, and brothers always fight. You needn't laugh."

"I didn't," said Terry, sullen and resentful; and indeed his voice was too near to match what Jo had heard.

"Someone did." Waist-deep in the water, Jo raised her head and looked about uncertainly. Her eyes searched the forest. Someone had certainly laughed; someone young.

"This is no place for one of your acts," Terry called crossly.

Jo didn't hear, though she was absorbed in listening. There it was again: a note of thin, young laughter, ringing like a bird call from above. *Brothers always fight,* said the gully, speaking into Jo's mind. With her feet caught in the ooze she turned too quickly, stumbled, and disappeared under the water.

"Jo!" shouted Terry. Before he could move she rose among the reeds, her hair sleeked by water and draped with vines, her eyes fixed on him but not seeing him. Terry looked round uneasily in case old Mrs. Willet had turned up, but there was no one.

"The brothers!" cried Jo, her eyes staring. "The blood brothers—they're fighting! Oh, stop! Oh, stop!" She put her hands over her face.

A trace of mist hung over the ledge. *Fighting,* whispered the echo. It no longer laughed. *Blood brothers . . . fighting . . . Brothers always fight.*

"Not funny," snapped Terry, for he had not heard the echo and thought Jo's teasing had gone too far. But Jo was shut away behind her hands.

"No! Not dead!" She screamed. "Oh, they've killed each other! The blood brothers—both dead!"

Always fighting . . . Dead, both dead!

"Knock it off, Jo. You're turning blue, and serves you right."

"Oh Balyet, oh Balyet," Jo whispered brokenly. "It wasn't your fault. You didn't know they'd fight. You're young, and the stars were bright and the brothers were so fine. It was just a game."

The echo mourned: *Dead, both dead. . . . A game, and the stars were bright. . . .*

"I'm going!" roared Terry, angry and shaken. He swung round and strode off through the trees. Jo did not see; she turned this way and that, blindly searching.

"Where are you? Oh, Balyet—so pretty! Don't cry! It was just a game to fool the old ones, just for a little while. Balyet, Balyet, soon everyone's old." She covered her eyes and cried out in horror. "But the brothers are crazy. They've killed each other! What will you do?"

A game . . . both dead. . . . What will I do? What will I do?

"Run away!" cried Jo, draped in vines among the reeds. "The hills. Hide in the hills! Quickly, Balyet, the old ones are coming! They'll see the brothers! Run away!"

The frail mist swayed above the pool. The echo cried, *Run away quickly, hide. . . . Balyet, Balyet, the old ones are coming! . . . Run away! Hide in the hills!*

5

MRS. WILLET, COMING BACK TO CAMP, had already seen the motorbike parked near the car; its sound was what had brought her back. She did not see Terry, for he was wary of the old woman and hid behind marri saplings while she passed. Finding the camp empty, she went on to the pool.

From behind came the roar of the motorbike being driven away. It might be taking Jo, but Mrs. Willet could not help that; since she had come so far, she would take a look. She reached the pool and discovered Jo among the reeds, half-dressed and decorated with vines.

"Come out of that, my girl," called Mrs. Willet. She was very angry.

"Gone!" cried Jo desperately, staring at her. "All gone! The camp, the children, all the young ones! Gone! Where have they gone?" She put her hands over her face and shuddered. A mist-wraith hung above the pool.

Mrs. Willet tugged off her cardigan and canvas shoes. In her overalls and satin blouse she strode into the water and, with an arm clamped around Jo's waist, began to drag her out. Between grunting and panting and fighting the mud underfoot, she chanted in a voice that shook a little.

"Don't!" screamed Jo, weakly beating at her face. "She's frightened! She's lonely! They've all gone and left her! She's not a ghost, she's alive, she's alive! Oh, Granny, don't send her away!"

Mrs. Willet only tightened her grip and fought and chanted on, until she had Jo collapsed and weeping on the bank, and could wrap her in her dry jeans and shirt and Mrs. Willet's own red cardigan.

The mist-wraith still hung in the mouth of the gully. Mrs. Willet paused for breath and considered what to do. She could not bring the car here, even if it were safe to leave Jo, who was now hardly conscious. She was too heavy to be carried; but she was chilled and white, and must be gotten to a fire quickly—and the fire had still to be lit. Mrs. Willet stood Jo against a tree, drew the girl's arms over her shoulders, and half dragged and half carried Jo on her own back.

She lay limp on the old woman's shoulders, only turning her head sometimes, moaning, "No, Granny . . . no." Sliding to the ground at the fireplace, she sobbed and shuddered now and then, and once cried out that the blood brothers were dead, but she did what she was told to help Mrs. Willet replace her wet things with dry. When she was wrapped in the brown rug beside a good fire she grew calmer and, little by little, seemed to come back to herself.

"Drink this," said Mrs. Willet, handing out a prescription of hot, sweet tea. Secretly she was still shaking with fear.

"I'm *all right,* Granny," said Jo impatiently; but she drank some of the tea.

"No thanks to those brothers, them and their bike. Didn't I say not to bring them?"

"I didn't bring them. It's a free country, they can go where they like. I only went to the pool to do some washing, and Terry came to see if I was all right." She looked about vaguely and saw that he was gone and that Mrs. Willet was breaking eggs into the pan. "I don't want any of those. I'll just go to bed."

"You'll eat a bit of scrambled egg like a good girl, or we'll have you going off your head. And you'll stay where you are for the night. I'll keep the fire up."

Jo, fire gazing, huddled gratefully into the rug. The little flames flickered, making the dark waver forward or back. Jo murmured drowsily: "She's alive, Granny. She's not a ghost, she's real. . . . She's so pretty."

Mrs. Willet bent over the pan. "So they used to say," she replied carefully. "You saw her, then?"

"Sort of—in my head, as if she was showing me." Jo turned her head and stared. "What do you mean, they used to say? She's your sister. Don't you know?"

"I know what they used to say. If I knew any more I'd never have brought you, wheedle how you liked. She's my sister because we're the same skin; I must have a thousand sisters I never saw. This one's just an old story."

"She's not! She's real. You talked to her, you know she's real; but you think she's a ghost and you're scared of her. Well, she isn't a ghost. She's alive, and she's so miserable—they've been so cruel to her—she told me—"

"Hush, now," said Mrs. Willet, hiding a shiver. "That's all gone. I was always sorry for her, but you can't put it right and you need your strength. A day at a time's enough. You eat this bit of egg and try to get some sleep, and we'll talk it all out in the morning."

Since she felt drained and weary, and the warmth was good, Jo ate a little scrambled egg and snuggled into the brown rug. Soon she dropped into a doze. Mrs. Willet cleared away the meal, collected more wood, and washed plates and pans. When she saw that Jo was asleep she heated stones in the fire, rolled them in towels and tucked them inside the rug. As the night grew more chill she crawled into her own sleeping bag, but not to sleep.

The fear she could not believe had become real indeed, and worse than she had known. The boy yesterday, wandering off and being drawn deep into danger: She had been able to cope with that. It was the sort of accident she had feared. But what had happened at the pool was worse; not like an accident; more like something meant. And working on someone's mind: that was worse. *She's alive, she's alive!* Remembering Jo's cry, Mrs. Willet felt a weight of dread that was almost too heavy to carry. Maybe this trouble was beyond her. Maybe there was nothing she could do.

All night she lay thinking and watching, getting up now and then to keep the fire going. When she had to leave it to find more wood, she kept an eye on the brown rug through the trees. Jo hardly moved.

Warm firelight, thrown up into treetops, met the cold, unchanging light of the stars. The hills overlooked its tiny flicker, gazing only at the stars and the far-off sea; but the sorrow in the hills, the sorrow that was Balyet, gazed hungrily down.

Starlight did not find her, for time had worn

her too thin. The narrow crags she climbed, and the steep falls below, did not trouble her, for she had no fear of death. Looking down at the fire in the forest, she reached out eager hands. Fire was life and every kind of warmth.

Where? whispered Balyet to the empty hills and the sky and the far-off sea. *Where? Where?* And she sighed like a soft wind, yearning over the fire. *Gone,* whispered Balyet. *Gone . . . all gone. Hide. Hide in the hills.*

There should have been men's voices singing like wind and sea; and children sleeping against their mothers, filling a girl's arms when she carried them to bed. There should have been young men sitting by the old ones, throwing glances at her when the old eyes turned away. There should have been laughter and talk from the women near at hand; and firelight gleaming in dark eyes; and always the whispers and touches, the teasing and soft laughter, of other girls near.

What will I do? sighed Balyet in her long and dreadful loneliness, mourning for lost fires and lost people. *What will I do?*

But now a fire glimmered under leaves in the forest, and down there the white girl was sleeping, young and sure and alive. The girl who called in the hills, who bathed in the pool and shouted with cold, who teased and fooled the old one and met the brothers, one or the other or both. Balyet laughed her soft, hollow laugh: *Brothers always fight.* Time, turning its great, slow circle, had brought her another Balyet.

Where? she called softly, teasing. *You there? Are you?* Wrapping her starved loneliness in mischief for Jo's sake, she hid deep in a cave and called again. *Come!* she called, too low for the stern old one to hear. *You come! Come here!*

"Balyet!" cried Jo in her dreams. But Jo was wrapped in sleep and did not go. Then Balyet grew sad again and called to her sister for sympathy.

The blood brothers . . . dead, both dead, and the old ones are coming. . . . Hide, Balyet, hide in the hills!

Jo stirred and moaned.

Where? cried Balyet. *Gone, all gone! Husband, children, sisters. . . . No one, no one! Balyet, Balyet, hide in the hills!*

"Cruel!" cried Jo, bound up in sleep. "So lonely . . ."

Lonely . . . lonely . . . Come! Come here!

Warm by Mrs. Willet's fire, Jo slept and listened and dozed again.

Toward morning Mrs. Willet reached a decision and crept out of her sleeping bag. Taking her flashlight and daring, out of need, to leave Jo asleep, she crept away to the old gray car and quietly opened the trunk. The rest of the food supplies were still there in the cardboard carton.

Mrs. Willet considered them. Choosing carefully, she took out an unopened loaf of bread, packets of flour and sugar, the container of margarine, several labeled cans, and the remaining eggs. These she placed on a shelf at the rear of the trunk while she lifted out the rest of its contents and set them on the ground near her feet. She unclipped two fasteners that held the carpeted floor of the trunk in place, and raised the hinged floor. Underneath, in its hidden compartment, lay the car's spare tire.

Struggling a little, Mrs. Willet lifted out the tire. In the empty compartment she stowed the food from the carton; then she lowered and latched the floor, restored the other contents of the trunk, and quietly closed it. The spare tire she hid under a tangle of vines and fallen branches on her way back to the fire. By then she was chilled, and built up the fire and crawled thankfully into her sleeping bag.

That was it, then; trick for trick. The girl herself was as full of tricks as a monkey, but Mrs. Willet didn't like tricks and this was the best she could do. Trying to fool someone made her feel ashamed. But what else was there? Talking and telling were no good; while the girl was full of young pity and young indignation, she would believe what fitted the way she felt. She must go home, get out of danger, and if she wouldn't choose to go she must be fooled.

Growing warm again made the old woman drowsy. She had not slept for two nights, and in the gray light of dawn she fell into a light doze.

6

MRS. WILLET DOZED FOR ONLY A FEW minutes. It was still dawn when she woke with a start and looked quickly for Jo. The girl was there, huddled in her rug near the fire.

"Hungry, are you?" said Mrs. Willet. "You never ate much dinner. I'll make a bit of toast."

Jo looked up broodingly from under the edge of the rug. "What are blood brothers?" she asked.

Mrs. Willet sighed. I'm too tired, she thought, I can't tell it right. After a moment she answered: "Nothing now. They were big business once, but that's all gone."

"Go on, then. What were they once?"

"They used to be young men from different places, strangers that met and wanted to be brothers. So they'd go through the ritual, and after that they were blood brothers. Forever after."

"Was that important? It sounds like a kid's game."

"That was big business. Closer than brothers, they were; they had to stick to each other. If their people got in a fight, and one of these brothers saw the other one in trouble, he had to go and help. Against his own people. It made all those people trust each other, more like friends. If it came to sorting something out between them, it was like having a man of their own on the other side. It could stop wars. They were sacred, blood brothers were."

"So," said Jo with her eyes on the fire, "if two of them fought and killed each other, that was bad?"

"As bad as you could get. You wouldn't even think about it. You couldn't think of anything as bad as that."

"But Balyet couldn't help it!" cried Jo hotly. "It wasn't her fault; it was horrible for her! She was in love with them, and they killed each other! And then all the others blamed *her.* She didn't *kill* these rotten brothers, she was in *love* with them."

"No use putting it on me, my girl," said Mrs. Willet. "I wasn't there. Some might say there was bound to be trouble, her being in love with the two of them at once and fooling them both. And her own husband picked out ready. You couldn't call that sense. Some might call it cheating."

"Oh, Granny! She's about my age—what would she know? How do you know about being in love if you never play around and find out? Everyone does it."

"They might now, but they didn't then. Girls were taught. It was all over by my time, all the old ways; I was brought up in town. But still I was taught what was right. At your age girls were grown-up. They knew how to live happy and safe, and not get their family killed or a spear through their legs. This Balyet had everything going for her: a young woman with a safe husband chosen for her, good looks, good people. All she had to do was grow up and have sense."

"That's what old people always say," Jo retorted. "Grow up; have sense. You know what it means, Granny? It means be a good little girl and do what I tell you. That's what growing up means when *you* say it: being good and doing what you're told. If people start thinking for themselves, you tell them to grow up."

She sounded bitter, and Mrs. Willet gave another tired sigh. The young fighting the old to prove they were grown-up: that was only what you expected. But this sounded different. It sounded as if Jo were blaming Mrs. Willet for what happened to this Balyet; as if, sometime in the night, she had taken sides against Mrs. Willet and put a gap between them.

Since she didn't know what sort of gap it was, the old woman only said, "When you're old you're no different; it's only the outside gets old. You're still there, the same as what you are now, only shut up inside; you'll find that out. Put a stick on the fire, will you, and I'll get up and make a bit of toast."

Jo fed the fire. "So that's what they did it for," she said, brooding. "Because she double-dated; just for that. You know what they did, Granny? While she was hiding up there in the hills, scared to death?"

"I know what the story tells."

"They all went off and left her: the whole camp, all her family, everyone she knew. They didn't tell her, they didn't even see her. They just went sneaking off and left her alone, up there in the hills forever. And the two dead blood brothers still lying there—horrible!" She shuddered. "Why did they have to do that? If she was really so wicked, wouldn't they have killed her?"

"They reckoned it wouldn't be right. The blood brothers: that couldn't be helped; they were already dead and their spirits gone wherever they were going. But they reckoned they couldn't send off another bad one to fret and worry decent spirits. It wouldn't be right. There was nothing like that before. No one ever broke the blood-brother law."

"But Balyet didn't break it, it was the brothers! It wasn't fair! Why did she stay? Why didn't she go after them?"

"Because no one would have her. She'd broken the law, just for a bit of fun. Where would she go, knowing that? Who could she go to?"

"But sneaking off and leaving her all by herself, for all her whole life! Just for doing what any girl might do! It's so cruel!"

"It wasn't then. Her bit of fun got two good young chaps, blood brothers, killing each other. It was bad trouble for everyone; it could've made a war, and that had to be stopped. What they did was hard, maybe cruel, but it was right in its time. This is a thousand years on, another time."

"A thousand years!" cried Jo, looking dazed. "But she's alive, she's young—I know her!"

"That's because she's so bad," said Mrs. Willet, stabbing bread with a forked stick. "Death won't have her, no more than anyone else. It wouldn't be right."

"Oh, Granny—she's not bad! She's just a girl like me! Anyhow, it can't be true—she's alive, and she couldn't go on living for a thousand years!"

"As to that, I can see you, can't I? And you can't see her. I told you death wouldn't take her; she's got worn away with time. Only, in daylight you can still see her shadow, pale and thin like a bit of mist. It's no good fretting, my girl—you can't change a thousand years on your own. Best pull yourself together and eat something."

Jo stared at the fire in resentment and disbelief, and took a bite from a slice of toast out of habit. Mrs. Willet gave her time. When the toast was eaten she said, "We've finished the milk and near finished the bread. Get fresh from the car, like a good girl, will you?"

"I don't want any more."

"Fetch it anyhow. We'll want it later, and it'll do you good to move about a bit."

Jo stood up unwillingly and stepped out of her rug into the sharp air. She went unseeing through the early-morning green of the forest. A long ray of sunlight, clearing the eastern ridge, measured a straight line to the roof of the car. Jo took a halfhearted look in the trunk and went back.

"There's no bread and no milk," she reported, draping the rug round her shoulders again.

Mrs. Willet shook her head. "Must be. I'll have a look." She went off, and came back still shaking her head.

"No bread, no milk, no flour; not much of anything. We've used more than I thought. Being two, I dare say." She sat down heavily. "Well, that's that. We'll have to go home."

Jo frowned. "There's still stuff there. I saw it."

"A few cans, that's all. No flour, no eggs, no proper food. We'll go home; can't live out of cans."

"Oh, Granny," snapped Jo, "of course we can. For a day or so, anyhow." She lifted her head and stared suspiciously. "There was a whole lot of food. What happened to it?"

"Used up, must be; it takes more than you think. Unless a possum got into the boot. They'll do that."

"That handle's stiff," said Jo coldly. "I don't believe a possum could turn it. I'm going to look."

She went off more briskly than before and was away much longer. She looked in the trunk again, and under the seats of the car, under the car itself, and even under the hood. After that she went prowling around the car and into the forest. She did not find bread or milk or eggs, but she found the spare tire.

She rolled it back to the car; it matched the other tires. There must be a place to carry it: She looked for a rack under the car, and again under the hood. At last she found the latches on the false floor of the trunk, and after that it was simple.

She felt astonished and bitter and triumphant. So Granny had crept around in the night playing this stupid trick, on purpose to fool Jo! The old ones! How cunning they were, and what lies they told to keep you under their thumbs. Like the lies about Balyet: pretending she could live for a thousand years, making out that she was wicked for doing what everyone did. But Granny was on their side, and she wanted to get Jo home. You couldn't trust the old ones.

Jo took milk and bread back to the fire and set them down with a thump. "You needn't worry. There's plenty, and the possums didn't steal it. You just forgot where you put it."

Mrs. Willet did not ask questions or pretend to be surprised, for pride had already stooped as low as dignity allowed. "That's that, then," she said, stowing the packets in the pan.

It was not enough for Jo. "Old people always forget things," she said harshly. "You can't believe a word they say, and you have to remind them all the time. Now that we don't have to go home, aren't you going off to work?"

Mrs. Willet looked at her with tranquil eyes a little shadowed, said, "No," and began to drag the fire apart.

"Why?" demanded Jo, suspicious at once.

"It's my camp. Today I'm stopping in it. That's all."

"You'll be bored."

"Good," said Mrs. Willet calmly.

It was irritating. Jo stomped away from the fire, stomped back and kicked at the firewood, swooped on the brown rug, shook it, and bundled it into folds. The old, dark eyes watched her, growing kinder; the girl was flummoxed, and no wonder. Only one thing left: try to show her what she couldn't see for herself.

"Stop fretting," said Mrs. Willet. "Sit down, like a good girl. Some might say it was you that forgot things, and didn't see other things right under your nose."

Jo turned on her. "What, then? What did I forget?"

"Sit down like a grown woman." Jo flung herself down by the dead fire. "Seems to me you forgot young Kevin, out of his senses and cold as a wet frog. And that howling you didn't like when you took him away. That was this Balyet, wasn't it?"

"I did not forget!" cried Jo hotly. "She wouldn't have hurt Kevin, she'd have loved him. You said yourself that she only wants someone to love; she just didn't know he was too little to go climbing way up there. Anyhow, I don't believe it was the same one at all; there must be two, and you've got them mixed up. Is that supposed to be what I didn't see?"

"Not all." Mrs. Willet's spirit-eyes lengthened their gaze, looking at nothing as she tried to collect her words. "You keep on telling me this Balyet's real, she's alive. But you don't have a notion what it means."

"*I* don't?"

"Use your head, girl. A ghost's one thing: it does whatever it does, always the same. It's not real, it's more like a mirror; you can tell what a ghost'll do." She paused to gather and sort more words.

"Go on."

"But a live person, now," said Mrs. Willet. "A person takes notice of what's going on and does different. A person changes; you can't tell what they'll do."

"So what?" said Jo, but Mrs. Willet didn't answer. She went on talking at her own pace, looking far off.

"This Balyet, now: The hills are her place. That's where she lives by right, and that's where I went after the boy. I knew. But yesterday—" Mrs. Willet's voice roughened, and she paused again to smooth it. "Yesterday she did different. . . . Stirred up by you and these friends of yours, these brothers. She came out of the hills. . . . She came down to the pool, where I thought it was safe. She worked on you, put that story in your head. Now I can't count on promises or what's safe." There was no way to hide the shaking of the frightened old voice. "God help me, now I don't know where she'll come or what she'll do."

"Granny!" At last Jo could see the fear, and it was real. It made her sorry for Granny, too. "Granny, listen: it doesn't matter where she comes. Balyet doesn't want to hurt anyone; she's just a girl like me. She's only dreadfully lonely and miserable, she only wants someone to talk to and play with."

Mrs. Willet's eyes had returned to Jo's face. "That's true," she said, "and it's pitiful. . . . A thousand years lonely, a thousand years hungry. For the girls she grew up with and the children she can't have. That's why she'll go after you and the boy, no one else. All she wants is another girl or a child to hug. . . . Only, when she does . . ." Mrs. Willet's voice ran out completely.

"Go on," urged Jo.

"When she gets her arms round them . . ."

"What?"

"They die," whispered Mrs. Willet, her dark eyes holding Jo's. "That's the story."

Jo gazed dumbly. Into her mind rushed a vision of Kevin, so white, just breathing. She could no longer shut it out.

"That's the most pitiful," said Mrs. Willet, her eyes spirit-dark. "That's when she cries like that. Crying for death to come and take her too. When she's had them in her arms and death's come and taken them from her."

"It isn't true, it isn't true!" cried Jo, springing to her feet. "It's a stupid story and you oughtn't to tell it! You can see for yourself—I'm *not* dead, am I? And you said Kevin would be all right, you as good as promised!"

Mrs. Willet nodded. "That was lucky; we got there fast. His blanket was still warm. She had to coax him all that way. And yesterday it was only that bike brought me home. She never got her arms round either of you. How many times can we go on being lucky?"

"If it was true," Jo argued desperately, "you would have told me before."

The dark old eyes looked into hers. "Why would I? You don't believe me now."

Jo walked about restlessly. "I do believe you. . . . I *believe* you, but I don't think you know. See, Granny, you just know this story; what they used to say. But I've talked to Balyet. Only I don't want you frightened, so I promise I'll watch out. I won't let her come near. Don't be scared."

"And how will you know if she's near?"

"I can see that mist, can't I? Her shadow, you said."

"You can see it in the day, what there is of it. There's no shadow at night."

"For heaven's sake, Granny! I won't be wandering about at night, will I?" Jo went on pacing to and fro, struggling with angry bewilderment. Mrs. Willet's story, and her own shocked vision of Kevin, would not fit what she herself had heard and felt. She was only sure that a girl like Jo had suffered very cruelly for what seemed a small and natural naughtiness, and that there was no one to take her part.

"Look, Granny," she said at last, "you want to go home: All right, we'll go. You're frightened, and I have to find out about Kevin; we have to go. But not yet. Not *just* yet—there's someone else besides us. There's Balyet."

"Have sense, girl. She's been there time out of mind, and will be yet. There's nothing you can do."

"I know that. But you said yourself she's a real person. And you said she's lonely, and it's cruel. I just want her to know I'm on her side. That's all. Maybe I can't do anything, but she talks to me—she talked to me at the pool, didn't she? I just want to answer next time, to tell her I'm on her side. Is that so stupid?"

"Depends, doesn't it? Some might say it's stupid to die doing no good, just to show someone you're on their side."

"But I won't die! I just promised not to let her come near! One more night, Granny, *please,* and we'll go home."

"That's that, then," said Mrs. Willet flatly. "I can't do more and you won't. You mean well, but you don't really know." She laid her head on her hand, deeply weary.

7

DROOPED BY THE DEAD FIRE, WEIGHED down by a trouble too big to handle, Mrs. Willet looked defeated. It seemed to make Jo responsible and in charge. She had talked to Balyet; she knew that, however dreadful or wicked the story might be, Balyet was lonely and loving and needed kindness. They could manage, she and Balyet. Jo was sure of it. She felt concerned and sorry for Granny, and just a little impatient with her.

She said, "Now, look, Granny, we've hardly eaten since yesterday. And I bet you didn't get much sleep, keeping the fire up all night. You ought to have a rest. You lie down, and I'll go and bring something from the car for lunch. We'll be better after that."

"We'd be better having lunch at home."

"You can't drive home on an empty stomach with no sleep," Jo declared. She felt a small touch of guilt, but she was young and on Balyet's side. It was better to be cruel for one more day to Granny Willet than to sneak away like all the others without a word of friendship, leaving Balyet alone in the hills, endlessly alive and crying for death.

Helplessly, Mrs. Willet lay down on the sleeping bag. She could think of nothing else to do. Jo spread the brown rug over her, fussing a little. "There," she said. "Now I'll go and find something good for lunch. It's daytime, remember, and I'll just be at the car."

It was good to walk off alone, with a little time to think, for her head felt as if it were slowly spinning. The haunting horror of Granny's story could not be pushed away. It made too much sense of Balyet's own story, and of Kevin's accident; and Granny's fear was too real. Jo found a can of stew and two eggs for lunch. Then, needing to make this crazy morning more normal, she climbed into the car to change her crumpled shirt and comb her hair. No wash; and they must be nearly out of water— The memory of the pool rushed over her like a wind.

She felt the coldness of the water, Balyet's pain, the horror of the blood brothers killed by their own clubs, the worse horror of the people all vanished away: silently, and with dreadful finality, refusing Balyet both life and death, leaving her nothing. She felt Balyet's horror when she found the people gone, and her longing of yesterday, and heard the echoing ring of her laugh. Then she heard, like a dream remembered, the calling in the night and Balyet coaxing her to come and play. That lasted until Granny's word *pitiful* broke into it, and Jo came to herself with tears on her face.

She climbed quickly out of the car: She must have been there for a long time, and Granny would be sure to make a fuss. Hurrying back, Jo had a sudden, clear picture of her little ball of washing, thrown into a bush.

As she came near the camp she called out cheerfully, to get in ahead of Granny's fussing. "I'm back! I just had to—" And then she stopped.

Mrs. Willet was not waiting in alarm. Worn out by fear and wakeful nights, and warm under the rug, she had fallen deeply asleep.

Jo stood looking down at her; she slept so heavily that she did not seem to be there at all. With her cheeks sagging and her lips moving slackly in and out, she looked like some worn old stranger. The old ones, thought Jo: Their weakness made you sorry, and then they grabbed you and hung on. Jo would never have gone back to the pool today, not even just to splash her face with cold water and collect her wet underclothes, if Granny Willet had been awake. Granny would have been too upset. But Granny

Willet was asleep. And the big billy was empty.

Jo set the can of stew and the eggs near the fireplace. Then, her heart thumping with nervous excitement, she took up the billy and went quietly away through the trees. It was only a kindness to bring water, and to wash her face and fetch her washing, while Granny slept without fear. If Jo happened to meet Balyet at the pool, if she could just tell Balyet how sorry she was, then the trouble would be over. Granny could have her wish and go straight home. And it was daylight, when the shadow could be seen, and Jo would take care not to let it come near. She would be quite safe.

A little way beyond the camp she began to run.

The pool lay in its hollow, as still and secret as ever, with the reeds piercing upward through the water and the vines draped over them, the ledge of rock standing above and the dark mouth of the gully behind. There was only a muddy, trampled place at the edge to show where Mrs. Willet had dragged Jo out, and Jo did not notice it. She set the billy down in the margin of reeds and gazed up at the gully. In spite of herself, her voice wobbled nervously as she called.

"Balyet! Where are you? Are you there?"

The answer came so quickly that a prickle of

shock ran along her nerves. *Balyet! . . . Where? . . . Balyet! . . . Are you Balyet? . . . Are you there? . . . Where are you?* The calls were everywhere; they ran to and fro, from hillside to hillside and up and down the gullies. *Where's Balyet? . . . There! . . . Where are you?* Now they were far and faint, and now so near that Jo's nerves jumped again. *Where?* they called. *Where?* A trill of laughter came ringing out of the hills.

"Oh, hush!" cried Jo in delight and fear. "They'll hear you—the old ones will come! They'll take me away again!"

Oh, hush! Oh, hush! sang Balyet very softly, in case she should frighten her new young sister. *They'll hear, they'll hear! Balyet, the old ones!* She came drifting down the gully, filling it with soft, excited laughter— And there was the white girl, below near the pool! She had come; she had called! Carefully, Balyet, carefully, in case she turned and ran away. *Oh, hush, Balyet, hush! The old ones! Take me away! Take me away!*

"I wish I could," said the white girl shyly. "I'm Jo." She was gazing up blindly, seeing only the gully. She said, "Do you have to stay here? If you want to go away, can't you just go?"

Stay. . . . whispered the echo, sighing gently. *Go. . . . The old ones are coming, hide, hide in the hills. . . .* A wave of warmth rose from sunlit rocks, and Balyet rested on it, weary with time.

Where is death? she whispered. But her new young sister knew too little of death, or of time.

Jo was silent, remembering Granny's words: That's the most pitiful . . . when she's had them in her arms and death's come and taken them from her. After a moment she asked, still shyly, "Were you dreadfully hurt when the blood brothers were killed? Were they very fine? Did you love both of them, or didn't you know which?"

Fine! breathed the girl who was faded by time. *Both fine . . . and the stars were bright!* She gave a small chuckle, and the rocks tossed it about. *A game,* she confessed. *To fool the old ones. Soon everyone's old.* While the rocks still chuckled, the sweet, ringing voice spoke again with simple pride. *Balyet . . . fine, so fine. Very fine . . .*

"I know," said Jo. "You showed me yesterday. You're so pretty." Though her eyes searched, she could find no wisp of shadow and her nerves still prickled. "I wish I could see you," she cried fretfully.

It called up the old game of hide-and-seek, fresh and new. *Wish, Jo!* sang Balyet, delightedly teasing. *I'm here, I see you!* She sprang with a breeze along the gully, calling, *Where, Jo? There! Balyet's there!*

The girl called Jo moved round the rim of the

pool, playing the game, searching farther into the gully mouth. "I can't find you!" she cried, and her voice shook a little from excitement or fear. The girl worn away by time was filled with loving mischief.

Wish, Jo! I see you! Find Balyet. . . . I'm here! The teasing softened into coaxing. *Come, Jo, come here. . . . Find Balyet. . . . Come! Find me!*

"I can't!" called Jo again—and suddenly grew still. What was that blurring the mouth of the gully? Wasn't it a trace of mist? Almost too fine to see, a mere shadow of mist? Stupid to die doing no good, Granny had said. Jo closed her eyes and opened them again; she must be able to trust them. "I see you, Balyet!" she called breathlessly. "I see you by your shadow!"

The mist wavered above the pool. *I see you, Jo!* sang Balyet in reply. *Come, then! Come here. . . . Jo, come here!*

Jo took an uncertain step, not forward but backward. She said nervously, "What will happen if I do?"

A game, sang Balyet, coaxing; but a shadow was growing at the edge of the game. She would not look at it. *Sister,* she faltered, holding out arms too frail to catch the light.

The white girl only took another backward step. "But what will happen?" she whispered.

And the shadow swept over Balyet like a sea; she was drowning in failure and loss, in endless sorrow and the weariness of time.

What will I do? she whispered. *What will I do?* And the whisper crept about in the rocks, and Jo knew that the worst part of Granny's story was true.

"Oh, don't!" she called, flooded with Balyet's pain. "Don't, Balyet, don't cry, it's not your fault! It's so cruel it makes me angry! I'm not frightened of you, anyway, I'm your friend. You don't want to hurt anyone—you don't hurt them, do you? You just love them. It's all these others, these old ones. They just want you to be lonely. It's the meanest thing I ever heard."

The echo whispered, *Lonely . . . lonely . . . lonely.* The pale mist-shadow wavered nearer along the ledge, and Jo stepped quickly back.

"We mustn't come near," she said urgently. "If we do they'll win again. I'm on your side, we're friends, only we mustn't come near." She made a small, pleading movement with her hands, not daring to hold them out to someone so isolated and in need. "That's still friends, isn't it? Not much, but better than nothing? I can come and see you, like now. We can talk. You can hide and I can look for you. If you come near it's all over. Finished. Like Kevin."

Kevin! sobbed Balyet in the deepest pain, so that Jo was shocked and shaken. *Kevin! Kevin! Kevin! Where is death? Where is death?*

"Don't cry, he isn't dead, he'll get better! Don't cry, Balyet, or the old ones will come! They'll find us."

The old ones, the old ones . . . where are they? Gone, all gone. Where are the children? Where are the young ones?

"Here!" cried Jo, rallying her. "You and me—we're here." She could not listen to Balyet mourning for the people who had been so cruel. "Come on, let's play. Hide again, and I'll find you."

Hide again. . . . whispered Balyet, confused. *Hide in the hills. . . .* Through the shadow of loss and failure she saw that the white girl was still here. Even now she had not run away; perhaps she had not guessed. *Hide and I'll find you!* whispered Balyet, and gave a tiny chuckle; it was as if a young, brown fist had wiped away tears. And Jo saw, with a little shiver she could not help, that the pale mist-shadow was gone from the ledge.

"I can't see you!" she called, anxious to keep the game going, while her eyes began again to search for a fragile scrap of mist.

See you, Jo! . . . Hush, the old ones are coming!

. . . *Hide again!* There was no way of telling where the echoes came from. *Don't cry. . . . I'm here, I'm here! . . . Play, Jo! Find me!*

"How many of you are there?" called Jo, teasing in her turn. She moved around the pool a little way at a time, straining to see farther into the gully.

How many, how many? . . . Come near, come over here! . . . Don't cry, I'll find you!

Jo dodged back and forth around the pool, gaining new upward glimpses into the gully, watching for that trace of gray against the darkness of rock. She was standing close under the ledge when her nerves prickled again: Balyet had only laughed, but now the sound did not come from the gully. It came from behind: from down here, near the pool.

She spun round and pressed her back against the ledge. "Don't touch me! Balyet! Don't come near!"

Touch me, crooned Balyet, teasing. Since Jo had turned, Balyet was somewhere ahead, but still there was no trace of her shadow. Jo swallowed a nervous giggle: Only little kids got worked up about hide-and-seek, or people creeping up on them from behind. She and Balyet were sensible people, and friends. It was stupid to panic. "I'll get you this time, Balyet, you wait!" she shouted, and went on searching.

This time, this time! Balyet teased from here and there among the trees. *How many, Jo? I see you, I see you!*

There was now no rock or water to make a dark background for the frail gray shadow. Jo's eyes searched in and out among trees, through patches of green and gray-green, down vistas of shadow to the shine of sunlight on leaves, caught here by a spiderweb and there by a twist of curling bark.

I'll get you, Jo! sang Balyet, back and forth. *This time, this time. . . . Don't cry, I see you!*

It was daylight, the safe time, and the rule of distance had been stated—but the mist-shadow was everywhere and nowhere, half-seen and always vanishing, making the safe time feel dangerous. The game went on, the tension built and tightened—and suddenly Jo's nerve snapped.

"I see you, Balyet!" she cried, cheating because she could not bear the tension.

And Balyet laughed again, a soft and teasing, a caressing laugh—from behind and above, on the ledge.

"Balyet, you witch!" shouted Jo, springing round in fury. It was mean of Balyet to tease her into cheating at a silly game like hide-and-seek and then to catch her out. The mist-shadow was just above, much too near for safety, and Jo stepped quickly back. "I did see you! You were over there! You must have run like a spider, or else there are two of you."

Two, crooned Balyet. *Jo and Jo. Balyet and Balyet. . . .*

"The same as each other? That's what I say!"

Brothers always fight. . . . Don't cry, Jo . . . touch me! Balyet reached out an invisible hand, but her white sister turned pink and stepped back. A silence hung between them; and into it the hills threw down the voice of the old woman calling.

"Jo! Where are you? Get back here, girl!"

The white girl said, "I have to go." She was still pink and flustered. "See you!" She scooped up the empty billy from the pool and went running away down the slope.

She was going, going! She was running away! Back to the camp and the brothers and the fire at night! Only one call from the old one and the game was over—so easily the white girl gave up her sister to time. Balyet ran too, as light as her own shadow, calling and coaxing through the trees.

"Go back! Go away!" called Jo as she ran. "Clear out, Balyet, she'll hear you!" But Balyet went with her, pleading and whispering, almost within sight of the old Clever Woman who knew the songs.

Jo! she coaxed. *Here, I'm here! Find me! Come, Jo, come here! . . . Sister, hush! The old ones are coming!* And at last, as she fell away behind: *Gone! Gone! . . . Where is death? . . . What will I do? What will I do?*

8

MRS. WILLET SLEPT DEEPLY FOR MORE than an hour, tired out by helpless worry and by yesterday's struggle to bring Jo back from the pool. Even her sleep was troubled, haunted by dream echoes calling to Jo, and once to Kevin. About midday she woke, sat up with a jerk, and looked for Jo.

There was no one near. The camp was still and quiet. The fire had gone out again, and near the ashes stood a can of stew and two eggs. Mrs. Willet dealt with the leap of fear by calling herself an old fool: Hadn't the girl said she would be at the car? No call to panic because she stayed there all morning.

"Dolling herself up," she decided, and would not allow herself to go and look. The girl would only get her back up if she thought she wasn't trusted.

Since it was now time for the lunch Jo had ordered, Mrs. Willet set about relighting the fire.

When that was done, and the can of stew emptied into the pan to heat, there was still no sign of Jo. By then the silent emptiness of the camp was more than Mrs. Willet could bear.

"We need butter," she decided, and allowed herself to go to the car to fetch it.

Jo was not there.

"Gone off on that bike, then," said Mrs. Willet, irritated and jumpy. Yesterday that had seemed safe enough, but today she knew more than she had then. And it was hard to believe that, after all that had happened and all that had been said, the girl would go off without a word. Mrs. Willet was shaken, and covered it by grumbling crossly: "Those that want a hot meal at midday have a right to be there to eat it."

She moved the pan farther from the flames and was adding another stick to the fire when her head jerked up sharply to listen. Whatever it was that had caught her ear, now there were only bird calls. They rang with an echoing chime, and she thought it must have been those she had heard before, in her sleep. No matter. Echoes or birds, the girl ought to be here. Mrs. Willet put her cupped hands to her mouth and called with the force of fear and worry.

"Jo! Where are you? Get back here, girl!"

She listened for an answer. There was none. She went through the trees to the car and called again. When there was still no answer, fear and worry forced her to turn up the slope toward the pool. A waste of time, she told herself; after yesterday, it was the last place the girl would be likely to go. Still: safer to look.

She had barely passed the fire and the cooling stew when there were sounds of running. In a moment Jo came bursting through the forest, the billy swinging and jerking on its wire handle in her hand.

"Where did you get to, then?" Mrs. Willet demanded, her eyes darkening as they fixed on the billy. "Just to the car and back, it was going to be. If I hadn't felt safe in my mind about that I'd never have dropped off, and the stew burning while I look for you."

"I went for water," panted Jo, with the evidence swinging in her hand. "We needed it. And I had to get the pants I washed, that I left there yesterday." Seeing Mrs. Willet's outraged face she added quickly, "It's daylight, so it was safe."

"I don't see any water," Mrs. Willet pointed out, grimly calm. "Or any washing."

"I—didn't get them," Jo confessed. She had no better answer ready, having meant to be back before Granny woke.

"Scared, were you?" snapped Mrs. Willet. "Came skittering back, daylight or not. There's hope yet, then; you've learnt some sense." Believing this, she was filled with disgruntled relief and held back her shock and fright. She closed her lips firmly, turned her back on Jo, and went striding, slow and heavy, down the slope.

Jo followed, resentfully silent. She couldn't tell all the truth, or certain people would burst a blood vessel. She was here, wasn't she? Safe and sound? Even if it had been a bit scary. While Granny was safely asleep, knowing nothing about the scariness, Jo had done the best she could to work things out; she could hardly wait to see Granny's face when she said, very casually, "When are we going home?" With Granny so prickly, and the stew burning, it would have to wait until after lunch; but that wasn't Jo's fault.

They reached the camp. The fire was almost out again. Mrs. Willet muttered with annoyance while she revived it and set the pan of stew to reheat. "Plates," she ordered, with the abruptness that meant she was seriously upset; and Jo, reacting with indignation as usual, dumped two plates down as though she hoped they might break. Since Mrs. Willet knew she had every right to be upset, she ignored this and became engrossed in breaking eggs to poach in the gravy.

They ate lunch in a silence unyielding on both sides. Mrs. Willet made tea from the last of the water and raked out the remains of the fire with an unburned stick. "I'll wash up at home," she said grimly. "We'll get packed now."

It was an order, and Jo's face darkened; Granny had got in first and made a fool of her. There was nothing to say; Granny would never believe she had already arranged to go home. Jo could only look sullen and wait for orders.

Mrs. Willet gave them. "Stack those billies in the pan and put them in the back of the car. That other gear can go, too."

Jo began sulkily, taking a long time at the car while she pushed her own things back into their bag. They no longer fitted, in spite of the lost underclothes, and she forgot to sulk in pondering this familiar problem. She almost raised the point while she gathered up her second load at the camp, but Mrs. Willet's forbidding face showed her that she was still in disgrace.

She was packing this second load into the trunk when the hills sent down the rumbling sound of the motorbike. Jo stopped to listen; she had an uneasy memory that Terry had been at the pool yesterday, when Balyet came. In the stress of that meeting, Jo knew, she had behaved in a very unusual way. It seemed likely that Terry had noticed, and she would have to invent an explanation. She waited, fussing with the things in the trunk while the sound of the bike drew nearer, until at last it came into view. Lance was riding, with Terry on the pillion.

Lance aimed the bike straight at Jo, where she stood by the open trunk. When she had jumped aside he braked hard and grinned. "Hi, doll," he said kindly.

"Oh—hi," said Jo. Something seemed to have happened to Lance: some glory had gone out of him. It was surprising to discover that, after all, he was only a few inches taller than Terry, and that he was the sort of person who aims a bike at you. She did not know that the pain and the danger of Balyet had raised her above smaller things. She was only surprised, and said almost mockingly, "How are the gold-tops? Still legal?"

Lance almost frowned. Since the question did not really need an answer, Jo asked another instead. "Going somewhere?"

"To town, for more grub; we're weak with hunger. I had to revive Terry with mouth-to-mouth this morning."

"Was that it?" said Terry. "I thought you were after my last bit of toast."

"So *that's* why you struggled."

"I'm surprised you're both still alive," said Jo. "Are you spending the night in town? I mean, it's a bit late: Can you get your shopping done and be back tonight?"

"We'll see," said Lance. "My idea is to do most

of the shopping in Mum's kitchen, but that may involve staying for the night."

"*My* idea," put in Terry, "is to see if you need anything too. If you're running out of bread or anything, we could bring it back."

"Thanks," said Jo. "As it happens, we're packing up to go home. Granny's had enough. So you could have the rest of my potatoes, and—let's see." She began to rummage in the trunk.

"Kind of you," said Lance, "but don't worry. We'd have to take it all back to camp, and after that we'd still have to go to town. I can't keep Terry away from the fleshpots for more than a couple of days at a time."

Jo took her head out of the trunk, the rejected potatoes in her hands. "Oh. Yes. Only it seems a waste—" But at this point Mrs. Willet's voice, sharp and rough as sandpaper, came cutting through the trees.

"Put that stuff back in the boot, my girl. Your mother never spent good money to feed other people's kids."

Sitting in the camp, counting knives and sorting food to be packed or buried, Mrs. Willet was tightly determined to be home before dark. Under her grimness she was shocked, shaken, and hurt. It was like a betrayal to know that while she slept, Jo had gone back to the pool.

After all the horror and struggle of yesterday—after the worry of the night, and the morning's painful speaking out—it was a hurtful thing to remember.

Hiding the hurt under anger, she told herself that the girl had grown into a stranger. There was no call, that Mrs. Willet knew, for anyone to put herself out for a stranger. Well, she had issued her edict and Jo seemed to accept it: They were going home. And this time it was for good and all; she would never be wheedled into trusting the girl again. "And that's that," said Mrs. Willet, and closed her lips up tight.

This fragile calm was shattered by the sound of the motorbike. It brought back all her dread, and the looming of a trouble too big and too strange to handle. The engine's roar came near and stopped: at the car, of course. Mrs. Willet dropped the knives and got to her feet. Suddenly she was shaking with anger.

Those two, whoever they were, those brothers! In spite of her they were here again, where they had no business. Messing about with her girl in the very shadow of the hills, stirring up trouble and bringing danger down. Whenever things turned bad, they were there—stirring them up, rousing that other poor thing, drawing her back from forgetting. She had been quiet all these years, until they came. They'd brought her back, and they'd turned Jo into a stranger. This time she would send them packing for good and all.

She came striding through the marri trees. There was the girl, handing out more tucker. Mrs. Willet called in a voice roughened by anger and fear.

"Put that stuff back in the boot, my girl. Your mother never spent good money to feed other people's kids."

Three shocked faces turned to her. Jo dropped the potatoes, which fell into the trunk. Fiercely Mrs. Willet called again.

"And you two, whatever your names are, don't come hanging round here bringing trouble. Get that bike away from my car and get yourselves out of here. I don't want to see your faces here again."

Terry was turning red, and his mouth hung open. Lance's was shut very tight, and his face was coldly furious. He lifted a hand in mock courtesy, kicked the motorbike into a roar, and went swerving away so suddenly that Terry almost fell off. Jo was quite still, frozen with shock.

"Well?" snapped Mrs. Willet. "What are you standing there for? There's more stuff ready."

Jo came to life.

"Pack it yourself, you old witch!" she shrieked, dragging things out of the trunk and hurling them among trees. "Talking to my friends like that! Telling lies about my mother! Who do you think you are?"

Mrs. Willet stood like a rock and gave vent to her anger. "I know who I am, and it's time you did: I'm the one in charge here. Maybe you ought to know who you are: You're a spoilt, selfish brat that could do with a good hiding. Anything's yours that you want and never mind who paid for it. Anything's right that you do and never mind who thinks different. I told you I wouldn't have those two here and I told you why: for your own good. Now you know I meant it."

"And what am I supposed to do about it?" yelled Jo. "Go running down the road and knock the bike over before it gets here? It's a free country—how can I stop the boys going where they like? You might like to know what they came for: to find out if *you* wanted anything in town, so they could bring it! They got a nice, grateful answer, didn't they?"

Mrs. Willet's anger, having exploded, was ready to die down, but this stung her. She said bitterly, "I never asked them, like I never asked you. Some might say I'm not the one to be grateful. But I'm through with dragging you out of trouble, setting you to rights, and putting up with your tantrums—worrying myself sick and having you go sneaking off again when I'm asleep. I'm taking you back where you belong for good and all."

Now it was Jo who was stung. "You know what's wrong with you, Granny Willet?" she demanded. "You're old and hard and mean and selfish. And miserable and jealous. Yes, that's it, jealous! That's why you're always picking on me and the boys; because we're young, and we do our own thing. You can't stand that, can you? You have to have everything *your* way. You're just like those others that did it to Balyet: jealous and mean."

"All right," said Mrs. Willet tiredly. "Now we've got that settled, we'll get on with the packing. The way we feel about each other, we'd be better off home."

But Jo was not used to accepting hurt and going on in spite of it. To her, Granny Willet seemed unshakeable as the hills. With tears in her voice, she cried, "Go home if you like! I'm staying here! I'd rather stay with someone—young and—lonely, and—loving, someone who can—play, and—be kind, than be safe at home with someone old, and—hard, and—g-greedy—" With her head down to hide her face, she darted into the marri forest, past Mrs. Willet and away up the slope.

Mrs. Willet's heart gave a great lurch, so that

its shell of anger and hurt was shattered. "Jo!" she shouted. "Come back, girl!" She went stumbling and hurrying through the trees, calling, "Jo! It's near dark—there'll be no shadow!"

But she could not run as fast as Jo, and there was no one to help, not even those two brothers. She needed help so badly, in this trouble that was too big for her, that she stopped in the camp to find her canvas bag; to open it with awkward, shaking fingers and take out the old skin bag with the booliah. Then she went on to the pool as fast as she could.

9

AS JO RAN, HER TEARS DRIED UP IN THE fires of anger, of humiliation, and of sheer injustice. She was burning for sympathy from someone of her own kind, someone young who knew about the unfairness of older people. Sunlight, slanting over the western ridge, struck the tops of the forest and turned the light to a watery green-gold. Jo ran through it without seeing, shouting, "Balyet! Where are you? I'm back!"

Because of her anger and hurt it was a peremptory shout. Balyet heard it and did not answer, for she too was hurt. She only drifted silently down the gully, above the pool, which lay still and secret in the green-gold light. There was the white girl waiting, the one who talked of friendship and ran away at a call; the girl who had no love and would not come near.

Jo shouted again. "Balyet, are you coming? Or am I going home? It's Jo! I've got something to tell you!"

Balyet smiled bitterly. Her sister was restless with anger like the sky in a storm, and there were dried tears on her face. Tears were quick-passing things, fit for short lives and a little time. They were for girls who were happy and safe, who did not know forever. Balyet called back a ringing mockery.

Feed other people's kids!

It was Balyet's voice, but it cleverly mocked the short, hard anger of Mrs. Willet, and it made Jo wince. "You heard, then," she said flatly. "You were listening."

Hanging round here, bringing trouble . . . Get away out . . .

Jo had to laugh a little. "Oh, Balyet, don't! Isn't she awful? A horrible hard old witch?"

That was a kind of appeal that Balyet remembered from long ago, and it softened the hurt. In the camps there was often anger, and after it tears; the fight, and then the forgiving—quick-passing things. If you have only forever, you need to snatch the quick-passing things. *Come, Jo,* called Balyet. *Tell.*

"What's the good? You know already. But did you ever hear anything so mean? And that was my own stuff I was giving the boys, and they didn't want it anyway."

Hard . . . hard old witch.

"And we were going home! We didn't need it,

and it wasn't even hers. She just can't stand Terry and Lance because they're my friends. She's jealous—a jealous old pig! They all are, aren't they? All the old ones. Jealous because we're young."

Young. . . . sighed the echo. *Because we're young. . . .*

"I know. She'd hate my being friends with you, if she knew. She's really scared of you, did you know that? So she can't stand it if I'm not too. Well, she can just find out. It'll do her good."

Stealthily the shadows lengthened; the sunlight shrank on the gully wall. *Find out,* whispered Balyet.

"Where are you? I can't see you."

Here! called Balyet gaily, turning her sister away from anger. *Find me!* She sped up and down the gully, calling as she ran. *Find me! . . . Here! . . . Find me!*

"Well, I know you're up there in the rocks. Come down here and talk."

You come! Find me, Jo! Come a little way!

"Don't be a tease! How can I find you when you're rushing about and I can't see your shadow?"

Balyet's dark, hungry eyes looked down at the white girl. *Come!* she called, with a smile that could not be seen. *A little way! . . . Quick, Jo! The old one is coming!*

Into Jo's mind came a vision of Mrs. Willet plodding up the slope. When someone has called you a selfish, spoiled brat, it serves them right if you act like one: Jo ran to the ledge and sprang.

It was not too hard to climb; there were clefts in the rocks, and a gnarled old root, and tough vines swinging down from above. In a moment she had entered the narrow mouth of the gully and slipped out of sight behind its walls.

Inside, the gully opened wide into a lofty chamber of rock, littered with boulders and brooded over by vine-hung trees. Scrub hid the western wall so that only its height could be seen, but the eastern wall rose to sheer, naked rock from whose heights the sunlight was reflected downward. Ahead, the walls closed in again; the gully became a dark, jagged gash in the hills, mounting by crags and ledges up to the flying cliffs. They hung over it high above: gold in the sunlight, withdrawn out of reach and leaning against the sky.

It was a grand and secret place, like some ancient, rediscovered temple. Jo gazed at it in awe. "Balyet!" she called nervously; and almost at once, with relief, "I see you! I see you by your shadow!"

She saw it only because it moved, a wisp of mist high in the sunlight on the eastern wall. Balyet climbed there, light and sure as a shadow;

patient with a thousand years of waiting, careful with a thousand years of need. This far, only this far, she had drawn her white sister into the hills. It was too soon; she might easily run away.

Carefully, Balyet: don't come too near. Draw her on a little way, a little way more—farther from the pool, the old woman with the songs. Let your mist-shape, hanging in the sun, show how distant, how innocent, you are. Long ago you could have held a sister in strong and loving arms, even while she struggled; now you have other strengths. Now Balyet is worn so thin that she climbs as the birds do. Now Balyet, poor Balyet, has no fear of death.

You see me, Jo! Come! called Balyet, filling the gully with mischief.

It was stupid to feel nervous and uncertain when someone else was so playful. Jo put her nervousness away and answered gaily. "What, up there? You must think I'm nuts! How did you do it, anyway? You're not a ghost. You have to climb, the same as me."

Balyet laughed like a happy child. *Climb! See me!* Her shadow bobbed and wavered down the wall until it sank out of sight. *Come, Jo!* she coaxed. *A little way!*

"No, thanks! You break your neck, if you want to. Do you live here? Isn't it grand? Like a palace." The wall threw the words back to her—and with them came Mrs. Willet's voice shouting into the gully.

"Jo! Are you there, girl?"

Jo froze and stood dumb. She felt clumsy and entangled. By now, Balyet's sympathy had cooled her anger, and running away began to seem stupid. Granny must have heard her calling out; Granny would know she was here, refusing to answer, sulking like a little kid. And in the end she'd have to give in and go back, and that would make everything worse. . . . And while she stood grappling with uncertainty, the rocks began to ring with mockery.

Jo! . . . Are you Jo? . . . You there, girl? . . . Jo, are you?

"Balyet, don't!" cried Jo. "She'll have a fit!"

Are you there? . . . Are you Jo? High on the rocks, Balyet could see the old one—the Clever Woman, the one who knew the songs and found the child—standing under the ledge, grasping at it in fear. But the white girl had entered the hills and would not go. *There, girl Jo?* taunted Balyet, full of malicious joy.

"Come back, girl!" Mrs. Willet shouted. "It's near dark!"

Come back, Jo! Near dark, girl!

"Balyet, you're making it worse. She's really frightened of you!"

You there, Jo girl? Near dark, near dark!

"Stop it!" shouted Jo, made ashamed by this taunting; but Balyet had broken into laughter.

Break your neck! she called gleefully, and sent into Jo's mind a picture of what she saw: Mrs. Willet grown desperate, struggling to climb the ledge, falling and lying in a tumbled heap below.

"Oh, Balyet, look what you've done! Now I'll have to go!" Jo turned to run. She had almost reached the narrow gully mouth when Balyet spoke from within its gap.

Sister, said Balyet very quietly.

Jo stopped dead, the small shock of pins and needles prickling her fingers again. Only moments ago, that voice had been teasing and mocking from far up the rocks; now it was right here. She had not guessed that a person worn thin by time could move so fast. "I wish you wouldn't do that, Balyet," she said fretfully, backing away. "You're not supposed to come near, and I never know where you are."

Here, said Balyet. She was not laughing or teasing now. In the soft, reflected light, her shadow lay frail as a cobweb on the rock of the gully mouth. It was hardly to be seen, but it barred Jo from going forward.

"Balyet . . . I have to help Granny. She's old, and she's had a bad fall."

Gone. The old one is gone. Jo's mind received

a picture of Mrs. Willet limping away from the pool.

"I have to go anyway. It'll soon be dark, and there'll be a fuss; police and everything. I can't stay."

Stay, said Balyet soberly.

There was no need to feel breathless because she had stopped playing. Jo made herself calm: of course Balyet wanted her to stay. When you loved people you didn't want to hurt them—but if you'd wanted them for a long, long time, you hung on to them and begged them to stay. You forgot to have sense, and other people had to remind you.

She said, "I'm not going for good, am I? I'll come back and see you as soon as I can. But Granny Willet brought me out here, and now maybe she can't drive home; I have to see. And I have to make sure that Kevin's all right. And Mum's coming home, and she'll be worried. How can I stay?"

Balyet answered earnestly. *Hide in the hills.* Like a child, she seemed to see no problem. *Jo and Jo,* she said. *Balyet and Balyet.*

"No," said Jo quickly, for the prickle of fear had come back and again it was hard to breathe. "People aren't ever the same, not really. But we're friends, aren't we? You know I'll come back." Tentatively she edged to one side of the gap: there was the faintest stirring of air, and the half-seen cobweb of shadow still barred her way. "Balyet!" cried Jo. "Don't come so near!"

So near, sighed Balyet, for the darkness was closing in. Her sister was held in the hills, away from the old Clever Woman, but Balyet must be cunning and patient still. She wanted so little, only love and a moment's touch, but instead she must play for time. If she won there would be one golden, lovely moment, one gleam of warmth and youth and comradeship—and after that, the long dark closing over, and the old, long sorrow flowing back. If she lost, the dark and sorrow would still be there; she would lose only the golden moment. *Touch me,* she whispered, impatient and pleading. But Jo backed away, stumbling over rocks.

"You know I can't," she said roughly. "Have sense, Balyet. You have to let me go." She looked in a hunted way at the bare eastern wall that Balyet had climbed so lightly, and at the rock-tumbled western wall hidden in scrub. A thousand years lonely, Granny had said; a thousand years hungry. People went crazy from being long alone.

Sister, pleaded Balyet, holding out her arms, but the white girl was afraid. She ran off between the boulders and hid there like death. There was no warmth or laughter; only darkness and sorrow and time, relentless as the stars. *Cruel,* sobbed Balyet, weeping.

"Don't!" cried Jo. "You know I'm on your side, only I can't *do* anything." She could not endure the hopelessness of Balyet's weeping—but the sun had almost left the eastern wall, and she could no longer see that cobweb shadow.

Gone, all gone . . . a long time lonely. What will I do? What will I do?

Jo took a shuddering breath, torn between pity and dread. She knew by now that Balyet, weeping, would forget the rule. Her arms must be reaching out, hungry and unseen, following Jo wherever she went. There would be no way past. But if the weeping stopped it would be worse: there would be neither sound nor shadow, nothing to show how near Balyet might be. Cruel or not, there had to be weeping—or a shadow—or a way out of this trap.

The gully walls rose to the sky, shadowed and forbidding. Above them, the golden cliffs were flying in sunlight; there was sun, if only she could reach it; up there, even a cobweb still had a shadow— And suddenly, as in the morning's game, the tension grew too tight and turned to panic. Half sobbing, Jo scrabbled over rocks and boulders, broke her way through creepers and trampled on ferns, to fling herself at the gully's western wall.

Sister! cried Balyet, waking from sorrow to excitement; for she knew the game of chase-and-catch as well as hide-and-seek. *Coming! Coming! I'm here! You there?* She laughed with delight, and the rocks threw the laughter back and forth until it filled the gully; and Jo, in her panic, scrambled up toward the sun through a tossing sea of laughter.

She sprang and tugged and gripped, not seeing what she gripped or what lay below. Balyet's voice went with her: above or beneath, to right or to left, excited or loving or teasing; keeping up the game. Jo heard without caring while she fought to reach the sun. . . .

Stay, Jo! I'm coming!

She clung to tough, thorny vines and swayed dangerously in space. She hung from a slender palm while stones slid down. . . .

Are you there, Jo? Hide in the hills!

Sobbing, she forced her toes and fingers into narrow cracks. With sore hands she gripped a rock and hauled herself up to a ledge. . . .

I've got you this time, Jo!

She was clinging to a crag high over the dark gully, fighting for breath, shivering with terror.

Panic had taken her a long way up toward the sun, but now it was over. There was nowhere else to go and no way down.

She had not thought, but had somehow known, that across this ridge lay the gully where she and Granny Willet had found Kevin; and that Granny, trying to reach her, might climb it as they had that day, and find a way across the ridge. As soon as she had breath enough, Jo filled her lungs and shouted.

"Granny! Granny Willet! Granny!"

Granny! called Balyet, teasing. She was somewhere just above. *Granny Willet!*

"Go away, you cat!" screamed Jo in angry fear. "Can't you see I'm in dreadful trouble?" Balyet laughed lovingly.

A little way, Jo! So near, so near . . .

"Balyet! Have sense, keep off! There's no room here! You can break your neck as much as you like, but I don't want you breaking mine!"

Break your neck! cried Balyet, and began to laugh. It was not her gentle or her teasing laughter. She laughed wildly, with excitement. Hearing her, Jo suddenly felt sick. She clung to the crag with damp and clammy hands.

Where is death? cried Balyet, taunting death and exulting over it, for this time death was on her side. One fear of it had driven her sister to this high, narrow crag, and another fear would not let her go. *Where is death?* cried Balyet in her triumph.

Jo shuddered. So the game was not a game but a trap; she had only trapped herself within reach of Balyet's arms. She should not have climbed. No one could outclimb Balyet in these hills; she moved like light, and, since death had refused her, she had no fear. The tangled scrub and the sky above became a senseless jumble. Jo could not look at them, and shut her eyes and laid her face against the crag.

Balyet saw and was sad. Her sister surrendered; the long dark and the old sorrow were closing in. But first the consolation, to cling to and remember through slow circles of time; a breath of warmth from the campfires, the moment of love and touch. *Jo and Jo,* she said tenderly. *Balyet and Balyet.* For she and her sister were one; both would love, and suffer, and remember.

Jo only heard that Balyet had moved nearer, and she crouched against the crag. In a little time she felt the air stir against her neck, and a touch as light as cobweb brush her hair. *I see you, Jo,* whispered Balyet. *Near dark, girl, near dark.*

Jo flung her head up. "Balyet— So lonely— A friend— You wouldn't hurt—" Her throat closed up and she could only look. No mist-shadow but something lighter than mist shimmered between her and the light: something that had shape. For a moment as sharp as a knife, Jo's eyes looked into Balyet's.

She saw the loneliness and the long sorrow and pain. She saw darkness and emptiness and a long, slow withering. She saw despair.

Touch me, whispered Balyet tenderly. *Because we're young . . .*

Jo screamed, clinging with one hand to the crag and beating with the other at the shimmer. "Young!" she screamed. "You're not young, you're old, old, old!" She forced herself farther around the crag. "You lied, you lied! You're not young and pretty, you're older than anyone—old and cruel!" She scooped up a stone and threw it. "You're old *inside*—a thousand years old!" But her words and her terror and all that she suddenly saw and could not say were lost in the crying and wailing of Balyet.

Old! Old! Old! shrieked Balyet, mourning and howling between the hills, for she had never thought of age. It was outside, and did not exist for her. All that she knew was beyond the power of time: the blood brothers lived in her memory, still fine. The stars were still bright, the people warm and loved and lost, her eager self still searching. Nothing had changed in all this endless time; nothing but her withering, fading self.

Gone, all gone . . . the young ones, the old ones, the children! Old . . . old . . . She had not known that her young self had gone too.

The rocks and gullies caught her voice and threw it up to the cliffs. *Where is death?* she cried, pleading. *Come here, a little way. . . . Find me, find me!* And then, sobbing deeply: *Old, old, old . . .*

Driven by shock and pity and hate, Jo sprang to catch a looping vine, and with it dragged a branch within reach. She leaped and swung with the branch to a slope of rock, and clung and pulled and scrambled.

Are you death? Where are you? Find me, find me! Old, old, old . . .

Jo's fingernails dug into gravel and grass. She dragged herself up, out of shadows into sunlight. The cliffs rose over her, gazing proudly across the plain to the sea, while Balyet's anguish tore at them and Jo lay winded and shaking on the ridge.

10

THERE WAS NOTHING MRS. WILLET could do and no one to help her; she was shut away from help as people are in dreams. By the time she reached the pool, her girl was already high in the gully and would not answer her calls. The other one—the poor, wicked creature—was with her, taunting in triumph and glee. At the sound of it Mrs. Willet grew weak with dread.

She could not use the old Clever song, for it protected only the singer; its magic would not reach far enough to help Jo. In a nightmare, Mrs. Willet tried to climb the ledge, to bring the magic into the gully—and found herself lying, shaken and bruised, on the ground.

The fall shook her back into self-control. She sat up carefully: she must not be injured, for there was no one else. She seemed to have only a jarred ankle, bruised knees, and one grazed hand: nothing to stop her, if only she had the strength. She took up the old skin bag that she had dropped and looked about in a considering way. She must try to get as near as she could, yet keep herself hidden lest the other one should draw Jo off again; and she must be quick.

The pool and the forest seemed like reflections in a mirror, for Mrs. Willet hardly saw them. They were only part of the ordinary world, which had no help to give. She had to reach past the ordinary world, into a world beyond. There was help there, if only she could reach it. Clutching the booliah she struggled to her feet and, limping from the fall, hobbled back down the slope.

There must be a place unwatched by Balyet; somewhere near yet hidden, where she could work. Mrs. Willet reached the mouth of the lower gully, in which she had found the boy Kevin. A single ridge walled it off from the other, and up the ridge ran the ledge she and Jo had climbed. It was not as near as she wished, but as near as she could get, and there was no time for wishing. She hobbled into the gully, found the ledge, and began to limp along it.

The limp grew less as she hurried on. She hardly noticed how she went, for her mind was fixed on that other world and on truths learned long ago. She had been a young woman then, young but staunch; and for her staunchness she had been trusted with the teachings of her people. Now she called up a vision of her teacher: gray hair and beard framing a dark, lined face; brown eyes, kind and knowing, filmed with age; a slow, deep voice. The last of the elders, keepers of the old knowledge.

Carefully, before he died, he had taught Mrs. Willet what he knew. There was no one else to receive the teaching. He had given the booliah into her care and taught her the songs. He had put the sacred sites in her charge, trusting her to tend them so that their stores of life might be released and the country might go on living. She had used his teaching only for that, and never as she must use it now. "Help me," she whispered, keeping his face in her mind's eye as she brushed aside vines and stepped blindly over gaps.

The ledge took her on and up: past the cave-like place where the boy had been; it grew narrower and steeper as it went. Sometimes she paused, gazing ahead and behind, unsure of how much farther she could climb. At a point where the ledge widened again, undercutting the wall as it had lower down, she hung the old skin bag from a forked branch and looked about.

In the shelter of the looming wall there were dead leaves and a few dried sticks, carried there by storms. She collected them, broke more dead wood from trees and shrubs that overhung the ledge, gathered fern and lily leaves made brown by autumn, and laid a small fire on the rock under the wall. When she had found matches in her overalls pockets and set the fire alight, she took down the skin bag and sat near. A thin column of smoke was rising; she blew gently until a finger of flame pointed up, and she fed it with twigs. Then she opened the bag.

Not the copper-green stones, or the blue, or the red-brown; those belonged to the sacred sites. With reverent hands she took out a small, glassy-black stone with a white star at the center and a red one with wavy yellow lines and two or three that were round and dull and black. She set these in a pattern by the fire, singing low and soft as she laid them out. Then, for the first time ever, she lifted out of the bag the large green stone, shaped like an egg and just as smooth, and set it in the center of her pattern. She let the stones and the fire fill her mind, let the song flow of itself.

After a time of singing, she knew she was watched from the other side of the fire. She stilled her fear and slowly raised her head: the wise and aged eyes of her old teacher watched her through the smoke.

She was warmed and encouraged, and fixed her eyes on his. The song flowed on until it was broken by the slow, deep voice of the old man.

"You have kept my trust, Clever Woman, and

now you call for help. What help do you need?"

"For my girl," said Mrs. Willet, speaking softly in case she should break the fragile thread between them. "A young white girl, just a woman."

The teacher frowned. "You seek help for a white woman?"

"It's black harm that's happened to her. She's gone to the woman of the hills. I was angry with her because I was afraid. That sent her."

"If she is a woman she was not sent. She went."

"A white girl, not knowing," Mrs. Willet pleaded. "Only turning to one of her own kind. A girl like that other one, but under different laws; to her eyes the old law was cruel. She is young, and the young are full of pity; then I made her sore. A girl in my hands. I can't rest with it."

"Sing, then," said the teacher, feeling her trouble; and Mrs. Willet took up the song again. His shadow hands, reaching through the fire, were spread above the booliah pattern.

After a time the song was broken again, this time by a cry from high in the hills: "Granny! Granny Willet! Granny!" Mrs. Willet, faltering, fixed her dark eyes on the teacher, for it was her girl calling.

"She is safe," he promised, "and will be allowed to see. She will come to you here, over the ridge."

"That's kind and good," said Mrs. Willet, thanking him with her eyes; but he looked deeply into hers and frowned.

"It is not enough. You are still troubled. Tell me."

Mrs. Willet shook her head. "It's all I ask. The rest can't be changed."

But his eyes looked into hers; and while they looked, although the air was still, the hills were filled with the raging of wind and the wailing and mourning of Balyet: *Old, old, old! Gone, all gone . . . the young ones, the old ones, the children! Old . . . old . . .*

"Poor thing," whispered Mrs. Willet, shivering. "Now she knows, too."

"Ah," said the teacher. "But that is the law, and the law cannot pity one woman. It must pity all the people."

"I know," said Mrs. Willet humbly; "I said it can't be changed." But the kind eyes, filmed with age, gave her courage to say more. "It's not right, for all that. This is another time, with different laws; there's young men and women doing worse things every day, and nothing said. There's girls like mine, and children too, can be brought to death by her, that never knew this old law. That's not right."

The teacher was listening. "Not right," he said, "but chance. Every time has its chances, good or bad, and we cannot meddle with them. Chance is its own law."

Mrs. Willet dared to sniff. "Well, then, there's the woman too, this Balyet: old and tired and worn away and still kept here, still yearning. And what's the good, when there's none left to know? It teaches nothing. I can't blame my girl when she calls it cruel."

"Balyet is old and worn away because she has traveled very far in time, as all creatures and all things must. Time is a law beyond any of us. It cannot be changed."

Where is death? cried Balyet in her pain. *Come here, a little way. . . . Find me, find me!* And she sobbed, *Old, old, old!* Her crying filled the gully and moved Mrs. Willet to argue.

"But it has been changed!" she cried hotly. "If she'd traveled in time like the rest of us, she wouldn't be here now! She's been *stopped* from traveling, caught in a trap. That's not meant to be—it's not law or right!"

He was silent, looking into time with his old, wise eyes. "Let us see, then," he said at last.

Mrs. Willet waited, hardly breathing, her own eyes dark as a paperbark swamp. In a moment, as though the teacher had spoken, she reached out and changed the pattern of the stones and fed the fire. The teacher began to sing deep and low, a song he had never taught her. She listened and watched his eyes and the stones and tended the fire.

The air grew chill; a deep, dank cold took the heat from the fire. There came a fog, or a whiteness like fog, flowing slow and heavy down the gully: curling and twisting, feeling its way, groping blindly over rocks with tentacles of fog. Mrs. Willet knew it from its heavy, clammy cold and was deeply afraid. She kept her eyes on the teacher's.

Are you death? Where are you? Balyet's voice came wailing. *Find me, find me! Old, old, old!* But the blind white thing rolled on down the gully, groping its way through scrub and vines, slowly thinning and fading until it was gone. The fire warmed again.

"Death refuses her," said the teacher, and his deep voice began to chant again, another song. Mrs. Willet felt the coldness of death still inside her; but she felt its calmness, too, and listened and waited.

She was watched: dark eyes were watching from rocks and among leaves. They were old eyes, stern and knowing; she glimpsed them and lost them again like early stars. The teacher chanted on, and Mrs. Willet's own eyes were fixed on him and the fire and the pattern of stones. But she felt, without looking, the many watching eyes.

There were more and more until the watchers filled the gully, a shifting, stirring crowd of shadows as restless as smoke. Mrs. Willet knew them from the teacher's singing: spirits of her people who had lived in ancient times; old ones who had framed the laws, and those who had passed judgment on young Balyet. When they had filled the gully and hung like the smoke of bush fires over the hills, the teacher broke off his singing and spoke to them.

"Greetings, you travelers in time. You have come far. Here is one, a woman, but old and wise, who accuses you of changing time. That is a thing beyond the law. Is it true?"

The shadows answered him, in voices like the hushed roar of the sea: "We change nothing. We only change."

Mrs. Willet did not look at them. She was only a woman, and human; she should not see spirits, ancient and wise, debating the law. She looked at the stones and fed the fire. The wind-voice of Balyet swept down from the hills, crying, *Death, death, death! Find me . . . find me . . .*

"There is another voice accusing you," said the teacher to the shadows. "Has she no cause? Have you not stilled time for her and left her trapped in it? The very rocks have worn away, and still she cries for death."

The hushed voices answered him. "We play no

games with time. We only refuse evil."

"And yet you rob this woman of her travel in time; you leave her no journey and no rest. Journey and rest are the laws of time. Have you played no game with them?"

The hushed voices cried, "She is evil beyond others! She has defied the law and the elders; by her folly the most sacred of laws has been broken. She shall not rest with us."

"Then," said the teacher, "you must find her some other journey, into some other rest. For we are all travelers, we and the rocks, the clouds and the sea; we journey and we rest. That is a law beyond us, beyond our land, a law of being. You travelers in time, you know the laws of time. You cannot change them. It is not your right."

The shadows stirred and drifted like smoke, whispering together. "We speak our own laws, by our own right," they said at last. "Though she is evil, yet we have given her one place: here in the hills. It is more than such evil deserves. She shall have no other place to journey or to rest."

"Evil is not the only evil," said the teacher sternly, "and we do not speak of place but of time. If she must stay in the hills, then let it be so: she shall journey in the hills, and in them she shall rest." Again he reached a withered hand through the fire, laying it on the smooth green stone. His deep voice chanted solemnly.

"She shall be warmth in the sunlight, frost in the shade, and movement in the wind; honey in blossom, poison in leaves and the fang of the snake. She shall speak only in bird song, hear only in rock, catch only in cobweb. She shall hide in the glimmer of water, and in sunlight or starlight cast no shadow. And this, her last change, will become the truth of Balyet; by this new making she shall journey into rest."

"Let it be so," chanted all the shadows, their voices hushing like the roar of the sea.

When they had spoken there came upon the hills a deeper, stronger calm. Mrs. Willet felt it. The last, late sunlight rested on the rocks with a deeper warmth; from the marri forest a scent of honey sprang upward as high as the cliffs. Something sly and dangerous rustled boldly in dead leaves; and from under a stone, spider eyes glistened as sharp as splintered glass. A wind came running light and strong down the gully, and a butcher bird fluted one strong, pure note that vibrated in the rocks.

"That's kind and good," whispered Mrs. Willet, raising her dark spirit-eyes to the teacher in thanks. He saw that now they held only tears and nodded gravely, and took his hand from the stone and faded with the other shadows.

Mrs. Willet took up each of the booliah stones in turn and placed it carefully inside the skin bag, singing to them while she laid them to rest as the teacher had taught her long ago. She sang quietly, but the rocks took hold of her voice and carried it a little way.

"Granny!" cried Jo, from above on the bulging wall. Her voice was ragged with shock and weariness. "Granny, is that you? I knew you'd come. How can I get down?"

"You'll stay where you are till I take a look," said Mrs. Willet, carefully putting out the fire. "No use breaking your neck now, and your mother not knowing."

"Oh, Granny, I thought I'd never find you! Wasn't it dreadful? Did you hear? And then—something happened. What happened? Is Balyet—gone?"

"Resting at last, poor thing."

"She was old," said Jo soberly. "Not old outside and young inside, like you. She was dreadfully, dreadfully old."

"Hush, now. Sit still, like a good girl, and we'll talk about it tomorrow. We've got ten minutes till dark."

The last of the sun slanted across the high, proud faces of the hills.

PATRICIA WRIGHTSON was raised in the Australian outback, on the north coast of New South Wales. As this was an isolated rural area, her formal education included lessons sent by mail from the State Correspondence School. Apart from that she was, she says, "educated by my father in literature, philosophy, and wonder, and by my mother in the social sciences."

Mrs. Wrightson's books range from realistic novels to science fiction and fantasy. She began writing for her two children, Jenny and Peter, and feels she was "very lucky to begin by accident in so demanding a school." Though decidedly Australian in setting and subject matter, her books are universal in appeal and have been highly acclaimed in her native country and abroad. Patricia Wrightson has received the Australian Children's Book of the Year Medal four times, for *The Crooked Snake* (1956), *The Nargun and the Stars* (1974), *The Ice Is Coming* (1978), and *A Little Fear* (1984). *A Little Fear* also received the 1984 Boston Globe-Horn Book Award for Fiction and, in Great Britain, the 1984 Young Observer Teenage Fiction Prize. In 1985 Mrs. Wrightson delivered the May Hill Arbuthnot Honor Lecture sponsored by the American Library Association, and she was recipient of the 1986 Hans Christian Andersen author medal, presented by the International Board on Books for Young People at a biennial congress in Tokyo.

After spending fifteen years in and around the city of Sydney, Patricia Wrightson returned to Australia's North Coast, where she now lives "on a narrow strip of stony ridge about a mile long" some miles outside of Maclean.